PALO DURO

A NOVEL ABOUT FRATERNITY RIVALRY
AT WTSU IN THE FALL OF 1969

Quantity discounts are available on bulk orders. Contact
sales@TAGPublishers.com for more information.

TAG Publishing, LLC
2618 S. Lipscomb
Amarillo, TX 79109
www.TAGPublishers.com
Office (806) 373-0114
Fax (806) 373-4004
info@TAGPublishers.com

ISBN: 978-1-934606-00-1

First Edition

PALO DURO

A NOVEL ABOUT FRATERNITY RIVALRY
AT WTSU IN THE FALL OF 1969

Eric Corbyn

About the Author

Eric Corbyn grew up in Ft. Worth, Texas, and attended West Texas State University from 1964 - 1968. After a two year stint in the army, he returned to WTSU and was elected president of Kappa Alpha Order. Corbyn remained at WTSU from 1970 - 1973.

Later, Eric Corbyn became involved in the specialty clothing business in Amarillo, Texas, opening in his own store in the fall of 2005. He is the owner of Corbyn's at 2817 Civic Circle in Wolflin - a men's and women's traditional clothing store featuring Vinyard Vines, Southern Tide, Southern Proper, Southern Marsh, Bill's Khakis, Allen Edmonds, Jams World, and much more.

Eric Corbyn

Chapter

One

The wind blew exceptionally hard and carried the first breath of the coming season. The freeze had come early this year, breaking all existing records for September and turning the huge cottonwood trees' leaves bright yellow. The wind tumbled and swirled the leaves around as if in a blender before blowing them straight across the quad on the West Texas State University campus. They would become the maintenance crew's biggest headache.

West Texas State University was not your typical school in America during the late sixties when every college seemed to be experiencing extreme turbulence. In particular, 1969 was a very chaotic year. The Vietnam War raged and its unpopularity continued to grow, sharply dividing the country for the first time since the Civil War.

Overshadowing the incredible event of landing a man on the moon, were the constant front page headlines of a strife torn America. Reminders of the shocking assassinations of Martin Luther King and Senator Bobby Kennedy were everywhere. The My Lai massacre in Vietnam, the arrest of Charles Manson in the horrifying cult murders of actress Sharon Tate and others, and the Soviet invasion of Czechoslovakia were just a few of the turbulent incidents that would set the course for tremendous change, particularly among the young restless college students who were desperately seeking answers to solutions that were simply not there.

During this period, music guided that change. No longer were the kids listening to the innocent sounds of the Beach Boys, Chuck Berry, and Johnny Rivers. Almost overnight came the psychedelic bands and the protest songs. The new rock stars were the likes of Jimmy Hendrix, The Rolling Stones, The Doors, Bob Dylan and many more. None, however, could catch the frenzy that a group of young lads from Liverpool generated- The Beatles. They were no longer the innocent English band that rose overnight to instant stardom by composing simple love songs with great lyrics and beautiful melodies. They embraced the new cultural changes with gusto and instead of mopheads, they became dopeheads. Even so, their music became more powerful to those caught up in the movement of change and their increasingly rebellious appearance added fuel to the fires for the restless youth. For many The Beatles soon became almost Godlike figures to worship and emulate.

This tremendous upheaval and change finally made its way to West Texas State University located in a small West Texas town not far from the New Mexico and Oklahoma borders. First created as a military school, it now barely resembled its former self. The R.O.T.C. program became voluntary in the fall of 1966, much to the chagrin of the local townfolk and also to the University's alumni as the strict codes of conduct relaxed.

The Vietnam War changed this quiet conservative Bible belt town for good. The college had grown from 5000 students in 1966 to over 9500 by the fall of 1969. Draft deferments for college students were still in effect during those years, which created a strong appetite for learning. The number of cowboys and farm boys enrolled increased substantially compared to just a few years earlier. It seemed that almost anybody of draft age in the entire Panhandle of Texas felt a calling to further their education.

The town of Palo Duro, which surrounded the university, experienced an upheaval not even imagined by their forefathers. The population, not counting university students, was barely 6000 and while the town folk reaped the financial benefits from the students for years, their attitudes had abruptly changed. No longer was the campus a picture of sharply dressed clean cut kids attending classes in uniforms as in years past. Now the students were a hodge podge of all types, appearances, and nationalities. As old Ted Gerald, the owner of Gerald's cafe for 38 years, had put it, "It looks like a Goddamn United Nations gathering around here," and compared to previous years, there was a word of truth in his statement.

For the first time, black football players were recruited from high schools in the North to help the University compete in its new conference. The new weapons assembly plant located 18 miles north of the town brought waves of northerners to the area. "Bunch of damn Yankees," rancher Red Pearson would call them.

Before the plant's arrival, the only heated arguments at city hall pitted ranchers and farmers on one side, against politicians and businessmen on the other side. This new order of things turned the world the townfolk knew on its ear. For the average resident of Palo Duro, the worst change they experienced was the onset of the psychedelic 60's - the dress, the hair, the attitudes, and the radical conduct that many of the students portrayed. As another old timer, Reverand James Peabody, pastor of the local Trinity Baptist church for more than two decades so eloquently stated, "My God, our town has been invaded by a traveling circus freak show."

"Hair, hair, hair. All I see is damn hair," fumed Sheriff Goodnight. "Don't we have a Goddamn barber in this town anymore?"

"Bunch a pinko Communists, if you ask me," was Charlie the local mail carrier's conclusion. "Be damn sure that we ain't givin' no more money to the Alumni fund. They can shut that damn hippie rat nest down and move it somewhere else."

Hair there was, and as each year passed since the Beatles invasion into the U.S. in 1964, hair styles grew longer, even sideburns and ponytails on the men that would put Elvis Presley to shame. The clothing styles that sported bell bottoms, worn out jeans, bright psychedelic shirts, and the worst eyesore that the locals had to endure, open neck shirts unbuttoned down the front displaying gold and silver peace symbols. To top off this shocking fashion statement were the earrings and funky headbands worn by both sexes.

"On men! Can you believe it?" blurted P.E. coach Tommy Taylor. "They look like a bunch of Goddamn queers!"

The girls projected almost as bad an eyesore to the local citizens. Only a short time back, the locals could sit on nearby park benches and watch the coeds attend their classes neatly attired in bobby socks and tea length dresses with cute bows and ribbons in their hair. Now very few 'Annette Funicello's' were to be seen frolicking about the campus.

A new and different look was in place. Sack dresses in drab colors were seen everywhere, and the dreaded miniskirt would make its arrival - some so daring that some professors had difficulty conducting their classes. Faded out bell bottom jeans and skin tight tank tops were common, and 'bra burning' incidents became a reality even in this small West Texas town.

These changes, which had already swept through universities on the West and East coast, came later in the decade to this small town, but nevertheless in the fall of 1969 they were definitely visualized and detested by the local community.

Even the sorority girls, who were thought of as conservative, started displaying this new rebellious appearance and attitude. It was now an everyday sight to see short miniskirts and sack dresses flowing barely below their hips, with t-shirts leaving little to one's imagination, as the coeds sprinted across the campus grounds to get to class on time.

It was a definite departure from years past, in particular to 88 year old Charlie Plow, the former mayor of Palo Duro who had been in office 16 years. For the last eight years since his 'retirement,' Charlie could be seen every weekday morning from 8 a.m. to 10 a.m. sitting on the same park bench in front of the old agricultural building where he once had taught, watching the world go by. His demeanor seemed to noticeably lighten when the girls would go by.

This windy September morning was no different. There was ol' Charlie Plow again resting on the right side of the park bench quietly watching the happenings about him, rarely making a gesture or any noticeable movement. But those who took the time to observe Charlie closely, could see his lips occasionally move producing a very soft garbled sound that was not understood by anyone nearby.

"Just mumbled mutterings," one passing student whispered to his classmate. "Poor ol' Charlie reminiscing about the past again. I sure hope I don't end up that way."

Charlie stared at the couple as they passed him scurrying up the steep steps in front of the agricultural building, but his eyes focused more on the girl's blue miniskirt which blew up and down, and side to side on this typical West Texas windy day, as she darted up the steps. The brisk wind was obviously of little concern to this coed Charlie observed with questionable discontent.

"What the hell's wrong with 'em?" Charlie mumbled out loud to himself, "Might as well turn the whole damn college into a French brothel." Charlie, without moving his head, glanced down at his watch noting the time as 9:15 a.m. Then his attention switched to the two students across the way that sat leaning against a towering cottonwood tree. The tree had been named General Patton soon after World War II due to its height and thickness. It was the most majestic cottonwood tree on the entire campus and for miles around.

The two students sat comfortably below it. The taller and better looking of the two continued to sip from a large cup between quick nervous drags from his cigarette. Placing his drink in between his legs, Winston Fox turned to his friend.

"Hell, Brother Pens," which was Manse O'Laughlin's fraternity nickname because he always carried a pen protector in his front pocket, "skip your class, don't be so uptight and predictable my good friend. You gotta smell the roses ever once in a while. Life is short." With that bit of brilliant advice, Winston lit another cigarette, blowing smoke up in the air to be whisked away by the wind.

Winston was a good looking kid of 24 years and had lots of character in his face for his age. He had strong jaw features, piercing blue eyes that would make even Paul Newman jealous, and his killer big smile always seemed to enable him to 'wing it' through any challenging situation that came his way. Winston's charm and his charisma were powerful, as his fraternity Brother, Red 'Cowboy' Slaughter would comment many times. "Winston Fox, you lucky son of a bitch, you can get away with murder."

Winston continued to sip from his cup and brushed back his long brown hair running a hand down his thick sideburns. He was quite the contrast to his best friend Manse's appearance.

Manse was lanky and skinny. He wore funny pointed glasses and his long protruding nose seemed to balance out his big noticeable ears, and 'those damn pens'. Winston often would ask Manse why he didn't get rid of that pocket protector, and also get rid of that silly out of style flattop and grow some hair to cover up his big ears. He looked more like he belonged in the 1950s than in the psychedelic sixties. Still, Winston always had a special liking for Manse and wanted him to do well.

"Winston," Manse smiled, "you know I'm not going to change. I'm never going to skip a class if I can keep from it. I smell the roses too, but they have a different fragrance than yours."

"Brother Pens," Winston gripped Manse's shoulder, "you are a good man and the best thing that ever happened to Kappa Kappa. I can't believe we spent so much time trying to ball a legacy as good as you. It was hell getting you a bid even as powerful as your Dad is." Winston chuckled, "Boy, were we a bunch of dumb asses back then."

Manse laughed and motioned toward Winston's drink. "Mind if I have a sip of your soda?"

Winston smiled but didn't offer the cup.

Manse arched a brow, "What's the matter, Brother Plato, you don't want to drink after me?"

"Of course not Manse, but this is not a soda. This is Boone's Farm apple wine, all 99¢ of it."

"At 9:30 in the morning, Winston?" Manse asked with a frown.

"Yeah, Manse, at 9:30 in the morning." There was a brief silence as Winston's mind turned to more pressing issues.

"Hell, Manse my pal, I'm depressed. The Delta Phi's, as you know, kicked our ass in rush this fall, 23 pledges to our 11, and as Chapter President I have to accept the responsibility. Our alumni chapter is going to jump on us like a duck on a June bug."

Winston stood up, pacing in front of the tree as he sucked on his cigarette. "We are barely rated number one anymore. The bottom line is that we're becoming has beens and fast."

"It will get better," Manse offered, trying to sound hopeful.

"It better," Winston warned, "or our chapter's ass is grass. Our alumni have about had it with us and we cannot afford to lose their financial support." Winston flopped back down and hastily lit another cigarette, "And to make matters much worse, our faculty adviser is being replaced by Tank Montgomery, who has just returned after a three year stint in Vietnam as a military adviser."

"You gotta be kidding me, right Winston?" Manse squeaked. His voice always jumped an octave when he was worried.

"Unfortunately, I'm not. I found out last night. Can you believe it Manse? The Kappa Kappa Generals, since the chapter started in 1949 have been totally invincible. The number one fraternity for 20 straight years. We've ruled the roost on this campus like Greek gods and now look at us. We're getting our butts kicked by the fuckin' Deltas - a bunch of Yankees mind you. Hell, Manse I bet a third of their chapter is from the northeast now." Winston paused for a moment, flipped his cigarette butt down in disgust and stood up again. "That Goddamn weapons plant had to go and ruin everything around here bringing in all those northerners. These damn Yankees with all their money, and their fancy cars, and their big fancy fraternity parties are blowing us away. Hell, Manse, our good ol' farm boys, cowboys, and small town members can't compete against them." Winston slammed his hand against the tree, "And all the sorority girls are lappin' them up like hunting dogs. Fuckin' gold diggers."

"Winston, I wish you wouldn't curse so much."

"Oh, to hell with it," Winston uttered. "Why does everything have to be so hard? Manse, my boy, we're going to have to get our act together and do something to stop the Deltas' popularity before the shit hits the fan. I cannot stand going in the student union building every morning just to walk by the Delta Phi table and see the smirks on their faces. Arrogant pricks. It pisses me off."

"Winston, it's not the end of the world," Manse got up and dusted grass off his trousers. "Sorry to leave, but I have to make my chemistry class."

"Just hang on, Manse, for once in your college career skip one class, okay?" Winston begged.

"I can't, Winston."

"All right, but at least hang around for five more minutes and then go. You can still make your class on time." Winston stared at Manse with what he hoped was the saddest face possible.

"Okay, Winston, but just for a couple of minutes," Manse relented.

"Thanks," Winston sighed, "no more bad vibes." Winston scanned the quad in front of them. "You know when I started here in 1962, everybody was in R.O.T.C. and wore uniforms part of the time. When that ended in 1965, the fraternity guys were walking down these pathways dressed up in blazers and stripe ties. God how times have changed since my two year stint in the army. It's like being on a different planet."

Manse nodded his agreement.

"Before I was drafted in 1967 it took forever to score with

a sorority girl, even the Eta Thetas were tough back then - couldn't separate them with a crowbar. Now it's free love, like a Goddamn petting zoo around here." Winston stopped for a second, laughing as he threw a kiss forward, "Thank you Beatles, and thank you, Rolling Stones for making my job much easier. It's like shootin' fish in a barrel now."

"Don't you ever take anything serious?"

"Why? Brother Pens, I say we drink up," Winston held his cup up as if to toast, "think of all the people in India that are sober. I think it was Shakespeare who said that."

"Brother Plato, you are hopeless," Manse shook his head at the same time smiling just a little.

Winston's smile faded. "Well look who is coming our way, Manse, if it isn't our last year's Kappa Kappa sweetheart herself. The little traitor Laura Love now in cahoots with the Deltas. Check those wheels out Brother Pens, they are longer than goalposts."

Manse sheepishly glanced her way, offering no outward display of enthusiasm.

"And look at that miniskirt flowing," Winston grinned, "Blow, wind, blow." And blow it did. Just as Laura approached a quick gust was too much for her outstretched right hand, revealing her bright pink paisley panties. Winston smiled with approval as Manse crouched lower trying not to look.

Laura approached the two, smiled confidently at Winston and said, "Well, Winston, I see you are being your usual industrious self today. What are you doing, trying to get as close to a class as possible without actually attending?"

Winston blasted her with his signature cocky smile that didn't quite reach his eyes. "Oh, aren't you cute Laura. When are you going to fall in love with me, sweetheart?" Winston dripped cynicism. He blew out some cigarette smoke that floated toward her.

Laura, planted one hand on her hip in an almost defensive gesture and asked, "Winston, can you even spell the word 'future'? I'm not sure you can."

"And Laura, my sweetheart, can you spell the word 'paisley'?" He glanced at the hem of her skirt. "I'm sure you can."

Showing no sign of embarrassment, she smiled, "Enjoy Winston, because that is the closest you will ever come to it." She turned and calmly sauntered down the narrow pathway.

"Damn, Manse, she really turns me on and she knows it, the little bitch." Winston paused as another girl drew his attention.

"Look whose comin' our way now, Manse, it's the one and only 'Screw Ella', excuse me, *Sue* Ella Robinson." Winston stared intently at her long blond curly hair and her cute little upturn nose.

"Winston are you getting drunk?" Manse was irritated at Winston's behavior.

Winston ignored him and motioned Sue Ella over.

"Hi, Sue Ella, you good looking devil you," Winston, even half popped, could produce a charm that no one could dare compete with.

"Thank you, Winston." Sue Ella stared right into Winston's eyes, then took his cigarettes from his shirt pocket, slowly removed one, licked it softly and put it in her mouth.

"Got a light, cutie?" she asked replacing the cigarette pack in his pocket, rubbing it gently against his chest before letting go.

Winston remained silent but stared at her beautiful green eyes. Sue Ella took a deep drag then blew the smoke out slowly rubbing on the filter with soft, erotic touches.

She then turned to walk away, "Give me a call sometime, Winston, and I'll give you a light the next time."

He grinned, "Damn Manse, this is what life is all about, like Janis Joplin said, you gotta get it while you can."

"And where do you go from there, Brother Plato?" Manse asked.

"No bad vibes, Manse, no bad vibes – don't forget – life is just one big escape."

"It's my turn to escape, Winston. I have to get to class."

Just then the President of Delta Phi, the Bronx stud, Michael Gentile, accompanied by Bambi and Buffy, everyone's favorite blond twin cheerleaders, strolled toward the tree.

"Hang on, Manse. I need a Tonto for two more minutes," said Winston.

Manse shook his head in a hopeless gesture, but agreed to stay.

The trio, walking arm in arm, approached Winston who by now had leaned against the tree with his hands folded behind his head. He waited calmly for the inevitable put down that he knew was coming his way.

The group stopped, and a smirk crossed Michael's face as he stared at Winston.

"And what might you three be up to?" Winston asked sarcastically. "Looking for the yellow brick road?"

"And what might you be up to, Winston?" Michael retorted standing in his typical 'Italian Stallion' stance with his head cocked slightly sideways. "Studying for an exam, no doubt!"

"No, Michael. Just trying to get a little fresh air. The campus buildings are starting to smell like stale New York factories."

Michael shrugged, his 5'8" statue flexed as he showed off

his muscle bound body kept in perfect shape from constant hours at the gym working out and lifting weights. He was not particularly good looking – dark brown beady eyes, large hook nose, short cropped curly black hair, and a broad snickering smile that seem to say, "I'm cooler than anyone else." Nevertheless he had already proven that he had a way with the women and his sharp Italian facial features were not very common on this West Texas campus so they attracted even more attention.

"Seems you Kappa Kappas," Michael mocked Winston's West Texas drawl, "got your asses kicked this fall or were you sober enough to remember, Winston, that we Deltas signed 23 pledges?" Michael displayed his trademark snide smile, "How many did you Kappas sign? A mere 11, I believe, if some hadn't already depledged by now." Michael continued to taunt, "Can't rest on your laurels, can you farm boy? You might be better off returning to your plow, Winston, but then again it's kinda tough plowing when you're already plowed."

The twins giggled, swaying back and forth in sickening delight at Michael's comments, like a couple of blow-up dolls.

Winston just grinned at the girls and gave Michael a stern stare. "What would a reject from West Side Story know about plowing? Why don't you go hop a New York ferry and go back to one of your New York street gangs where you belong?"

Michael's head drew back as Winston's remarks hit a sore spot. "Why I ought to," Michael started to head for Winston, but was stopped by the twins who each grabbed an arm.

"Ignore him, Michael," Bambi said, or maybe it was Buffy, Winston never could tell them apart.

Michael stood his ground, the left side of his upper lip quivering.

"Been watching too many Elvis Presley movies lately,

stallion breath?" Winston asked, taking one last sip from his cup. "Remember, quality, not quantity, is the name of the game. You Deltas remind me of a rabbit farm."

"Yeah, right, farm boy. If you are supposed to be an example of quality, then you Kappas got some major problems."

"Come on, Michael, we're going to be late for our classes," Bambi urged pulling Michael gently away.

"Time for basket weaving no doubt girls?" Winston asked. "Maybe with a little bit of luck you will find a bubble gum machine along the way."

"Screw you, Winston," Michael gave him one final glare "Drink up, farm boy, because the Kappa Kappas are history." Michael, with one twin on each arm, backed away and headed for the Ag building. During the whole exchange, Manse sat restlessly next to Winston constantly checking his watch.

Winston watched the trio approach the steep steps, stood up and hollered out to Michael mocking his New York Italian accent, "Be careful, Michael, because there are lions, tigers, and Kappas out here and they are coming to get you."

"Bye, Winston," Manse jumped up and ran down the pathway heading for his class.

Winston turned around just in time to see his girlfriend Gloria approach. *Damn*, Winston thought. *She is going to know I skipped my 9:00 accounting class.* Her bright red and white striped dress clung to her curves with the help of the wind showing every detail.

"Hi, Gloria," Winston greeted her, "What are you doing here so early? Your English class isn't for another hour."

Instead of stopping, she kept walking with Winston following close behind.

"What's the matter, Gloria?" Winston asked already sensing her answer. "What's wrong?"

"Oh, Winston, take a big guess," she blurted continuing her brisk pace, "just leave me alone. I'm on my way to the library."

"Are you mad at me?" Winston asked, hoping his sad blue eyes would encourage sympathy from Gloria but she wouldn't even look at him.

"No, Winston, I'm not mad, just forever disappointed in you." Gloria shook her head, "It's the same old thing, promises and more promises, and none ever kept - the same old broken record. You told me this semester you wouldn't skip any classes unless it was absolutely necessary. And here you sit blowing off your 9:00 a.m. accounting class. How many others have there been?" Gloria kept walking, her pace increasing as she spoke.

"Winston, I love you, but I'm tired of being your mother. I give up. I graduate in four months - then what? Sit around and teach for God knows how long, waiting for you to finish your decade-long college career?" Gloria stopped and turned toward him, tears running down her face. She gave Winston a long hug. "Please, Winston for your own sake, do something with yourself."

Winston said nothing just stared at Gloria with total admiration. *Damn,* he thought to himself, Gloria was so beautiful and such a wonderful person. He kept staring at her tall, lean frame. Her striking hazel eyes kept him mesmerized as did those magnificent long legs.

Gloria remained silent as she flipped her long brown hair away from her face. She looked as if she was trying to figure out what was going on in his mind.

Winston kept staring at Gloria in total awe knowing that her greatest asset was not her beauty, but her loving mind. Everybody that was around her knew she had a kind heart, a loving disposition and a calming way that no one could touch.

She doesn't need me, Winston told himself. *You dumb shit, you are going to blow this one too.*

"Winston, what are you thinking?" Gloria asked.

"Nothing, just a bit depressed over rush this fall," Winston shoved his hands in his pockets. "Those damn Deltas really put it to us this time."

"Winston," Gloria tilted her head and glared, " are we going to live our lives in a fraternal haze from now on? Believe it or not, fraternity life at West Texas State University is not the center of the universe. Five years from now nobody will even remember what happened, and not only that, most of them will not even care."

"I will," was all Winston said, disappointed that she didn't understand.

Winston walked quietly away and Gloria started to speak, but instead watched him disappear around the corner. *Where are we going to be this time next year?* Gloria wondered as she walked up the stone steps to the library. *I don't even want to know.*

Chapter

Two

"Order please!" The President of Kappa Kappa, Winston Fox, demanded banging his gavel on his desk repeatedly. The noise echoed around the Kappa Kappa meeting room. Winston knew that this meeting was going to be a lot more serious than others before. His usual easy going manner was not present tonight. Instead, a frown creased his brow as he nervously rubbed his left sideburn.

"What's wrong with Brother Plato?" One of the members whispered.

"I think we are fixin' to find out," Came an answer from a couple of rows back.

Winston cleared his throat, "My fellow Kappas, as of now the formality of our meeting has ended. In five minutes, our new faculty adviser retired Brigadier General Tank

Montgomery, whom we all know too well from three years back, will address our chapter. As you know, or might have heard, he has just returned from a three year stint as a military consultant in Vietnam. What he is going to say, I don't know for sure," Winston paused stood up, lit a cigarette, took a deep drag and then proceeded, "but it is my intelligent guess that we Kappas are in deep shit." Gasps could be heard through the room followed by rapid chattering and whispering.

Winston again pounded the desk with his gavel. "Will you all please shut up? This is serious shit this time. I'm warning you no snickering, making funny faces, or whispering when he speaks. If we lose our alumni's financial backing, this chapter is history."

Suddenly to Winston's left, the room's metal door flung open. There in the doorway stood the ominous figure of J. William Tank Montgomery.

"Oh, God, is he not scary? He makes Patton look like Pat Boone," one of the members whispered in a low voice.

"Shut up Charlie, he can hear you - he's got ears like a coyote," another whispered.

The general took two military steps forward and stopped. His commanding presence was awesome. He looked as though he was about to lead troops into battle. Tank was now 74 years old but no one could tell it - he looked at least 15 years younger. He was a towering figure - standing 6'4," weighing 250 pounds. He wore a khaki shirt, khaki riding pants that ballooned out at the thighs and leather riding boots that laced almost to his knees. In his right hand he held a leather swagger stick, which he constantly popped against his right leg, as if he was irritated and just waiting for an excuse to whack someone.

Tank's face had weathered through the tough years in combat. The wrinkles had deepened, his eyes and his big nose had reddened but under those grey bushy eyebrows were two beady eyes that could stare down a mountain lion - they literally sent chills down the spine with their intensity. He sported an ever present flattop and his signature cigar clenched tightly in the left corner of his mouth. The cigar crunched as he chewed the end.

"I've seen labs chew on bones quieter than that," Winston whispered to Manse.

The General stood like a statue making no attempt to speak or move forward, but his beady eyes darted back and forth zeroing in on the members in turn while he repeatedly slapped his right leg with his swagger stick.

The chapter room had fallen into complete silence. Not one soul moved or made a sound. They all sat like scared little schoolboys who were about to be popped by a nun with a ruler. Finally, the chapter's Sergeant at Arms meekly approached the General.

"General, sir," his voice quivered. "With all due respect, you know the rules. I cannot allow you to enter our chapter room without you reentering, sir, and giving the secret knock."

Winston shook his head from left to right in dismay. "Brother Perry," Winston mumbled, "I don't think I would have said that."

"Like hell you won't, boy!" The General growled with a gruff voice as heavy as molasses. His flattop bristled like a cat's back. "The only knock I'm going to give is when I knock a few heads across this chapter floor. Get the message, boy?"

"Holy shit, we're in trouble now," mumbled Brother Cowboy.

"Sh, sh, shhhh," came a chorus of whispers back to him.

The general, his face as red as a boiling lobster, marched toward the chapter officer's table. Winston made a point not to show any outward signs that he might be intimidated by the general's actions, and offered his hand for the General's to shake. "Good evening, sir, we are so proud…"

The general cut him off, "Let's cut the crap, President Fox. I did not come here to play patty cake." The general stood by the microphone like a military statue, except for his penetrating eyes which darted from side to side as he stared down his captive audience.

"God, this is getting scary," a voice from the second row whispered, "He's not even slapping his swagger stick on his leg."

"Damn it, Sgt. T., shut up, Brother Roll'em Rick warned softly, "Tank can read lips better than anyone."

The general's trance continued, like a person that is seconds away from dying. Before he knew it, the General's whole life sped through his mind in a matter of a few seconds. Newsreels flashed before his eyes - there he was riding tanks with General Patton in the final days of World War II, nearly getting blown to pieces near the 38th parallel in Korea, and then the four chopper crashes he managed to survive in Vietnam. Every shell, every bomb, every wound, every major triumph and every major disappointment in his long military career rolled through his memory in fast motion. Tank momentarily pulling his cigar from the corner of his mouth and relit it. Then, biting and chewing it at the same time, the General's mind flashed back to 1952 when he was standing in this very same chapter room, as the Kappa Kappa faculty advisor.

"Here we go again," Brother Rodeo Cool mumbled.

"Sh, sh, shhh," again was whispered from several of the members.

Tank spent a moment on the memory of that moment. *There I was standing behind this very same oak table presiding over 34 of the finest military specimens that any army commander could ever had hoped to lead into battle. God, we looked good,* the General congratulated himself. *All dressed to perfection in our uniforms - 34 of the finest Kappas ever assembled in one chapter room.*

Tank puffed hard on his cigar and he managed to show a meager smile, but it was short lived as again he focused his piercing stare on the new chapter members that sat before him.

"What the fuck is wrong with this dude?" Roll'em Rick whispered so quietly that only Manse sitting next to him could hear, "Is he on drugs?"

Without warning, Tank slammed his swagger stick on the oak table so hard that it almost snapped in half. The members jumped in their chairs in unison. Smoke poured from Tank's ears, or maybe it was from his cigar, nobody wanted to find out for sure.

"You," the general pointed his swagger stick toward the second row, "that's right clown, you with the Fu Manchu beard and that silly red flowered shirt, stand up."

Slowly Roll'em Rick sheepishly stood, his head bowed and his knees visibly shaking.

"What was that smart ass remark, boy?" Tank asked. "Am I on drugs? Was that it? Is that correct? Speak up!" Tank demanded.

"Sir, in all due respect, I didn't mean…"

"Sit back down and shut up!" Tank demanded, then paced back and forth. "Gentlemen, and I use that term loosely, I stand here gazing out at the Kappas before me and what do you think I see?" Tank paused for a second shaking his head in disgust. "Do I see strong military minded men displaying strong leadership qualities? Hell, no! Instead what do I see?"

The general slammed his swagger stick hard on the oak desk. "Look at you: flowered shirts, filthy worn out jeans, and,

my God, even sandals. Christ you look like a Goddamn freak
show. Hell, Ringling Brothers' Circus wouldn't even take
you in. Pathetic, mind you, absolutely pathetic." Tank walked
over to the north wall where four large oil portraits hung side
by side. "As you can see, my fellow Brothers," Tank trying
to calm himself down, softened his voice, "these four fine
military generals - George Washington, Harry Lighthorse Lee,
Stonewall Jackson, and last but not least, the great general
Robert E. Lee, are the reasons this fraternity was formed at
Washington and Lee in 1877.

Not only are we to respect and honor them, we are to emulate
them in the best Kappa Kappa manner possible. "Remember
our motto, Brothers, 'Integrity, honor, and country.' I will say
no more." The general now seemingly more relaxed, returned
to the table and sat down, puffing heavily on his cigar and
sending an occasional circle up in the air.

"Like Indian smoke signals," Winston observed, "that is
not a good omen."

"My fellow Kappas," the general said, "I have come here
tonight on behalf of our distinguished alumni association at
West Texas State University to relay a few changes that are
going to take place this current fall semester." Tank paused for
a second and then a big grin crossed his face. "Allow me to be
more specific. First, we will address chapter finances. As you
well know your generous alumni pump $4,500 dollars every
semester into the chapter's treasury."

Tank reached into his shirt pocket and pulled out a small
notebook. Putting on his reading glasses, he started his
inevitable onslaught, "It has been brought to my attention that
as of September 23rd, only two of Kappa Kappa's members
are current on their dues out of a total membership of 59. Of
course we know who these two are, don't we?" Tank smirked
with pleasure, "None other than Brother Manse O'Laughlin
and, thanks to his trust fund, Brother Charlie Spoon Luna."

Tank continued, "Next subject - academics. Last spring you missed probation by the hair on your chinny chin chin. If it were not for Brother Manse's 21 hours with a perfect 4.0, you clowns would already be history." Tank stood and paced around his face glowing red as if he could hardly contain his anger. He stopped and once again slammed his stick again hard on the table.

"Eight years ago, gentlemen, this chapter had an overall 3.4 grade average – the highest of all our chapters in the nation. Since 1949 we have ruled the roost around here – rated number one fraternity on campus – nobody could touch us. The way I figure it, if the Deltas kick your asses one more time in the next spring rush – that status will end after decades of work." Tank shook his head and sat down. "My fellow classmate and former retired F.B.I. agent, Brother Randolph Churchill has taken the time to do a little investigative work for me during my absence to see what exactly has been going on around here." He allowed an almost evil expression to cross his face.

"Uh oh," said Brother Red Cowboy Slaughter, "Here she comes."

"Gentlemen, the following facts, brought to my attention by Brother Churchill, are most disturbing. At the end of last spring semester our chapter membership was reduced by 14 members – none, mind you, because of graduation. On the contrary, we lost eight for flunking out, three by behavior suspension, and three members lost their lives, not dying for their country in Vietnam, but dying in other, largely preventable, ways."

"The shit is fixin' to hit the fan, man," Roll'em Rick commented shaking his head in hopelessness.

"Our first Brother to meet an unfortunate and untimely death was Fridge Gilliland, all 338 pounds of him. Our All-American guard in his junior year – unfortunately, he was killed while engaging in extensive headon tackling." Tank stopped for a minute and gave a disgusted sigh, "The only problem was that this did not occur during football practice, but instead Brother Fridge, in a drunken stupor decided to take a 23 car Santa Fe train head on, roaring down the tracks in his 1962 Ford at an incredible speed. Nobody as yet has been able to find all of his remains."

"Our second untimely death to one of our Brothers was none other than Brother Bo Peep himself, who fell four stories to his death." The general paused and flipped his long ash into the nearby water glass. "Did he fall from a grain elevator while engaged in respected employment? Not hardly. Instead, as you all know, he fell from the fourth floor of the Zeta's sorority house as he attempted to peek into a shower window. And our final Brother who passed away this year was Brother Mole, whose death was the most horrible of all," Tank paused as if completely disgusted. "Brother Mole spent the better part of a finals night rummaging through the dumpster behind the science building looking for a chemistry exam only to pass out later not knowing that it would be a permanent sleep. The next morning the trash truck crushed him to pieces. The autopsy report was no surprise – marijuana, alcohol, and God knows what else was discovered in his blood." Tank stopped and asked, "Are we having fun yet?" Tank turned another page in his notebook and continued.

"Three more final incidents, gentlemen, and we'll call it a night. First, Brother Fig Newton, suspended for two semesters for running through the Florence Nightingale in his underwear, drunk of course, spraying the girls' pajama tops with a seltzer bottle."

"Second, our dear Brother Alke, once the University's starting quarterback before he became a lush, was caught dressed up as a visiting women's basketball coach, as he, or should I say she, roamed the locker room and shower area. Suspension for two semesters." Tank eyes turned redder by the minute, and his big red bulb-like nose brought on from years of gin martinis looked like it was about to explode.

"And our third and final incident to report," Tank was interrupted by several members hollering and clapping. "You misfits cut it out right now or I will keep you here 'til hell freezes over," he growled. "Do I make myself perfectly clear?"

"Yes, sir," replied the chapter members in low voices.

"I can't hear you," Tank yelled.

"YES, SIR!" the members yelled out this time with more enthusiasm.

"That's better, and as I was saying Brother Beerwolf who has the dubious pleasure of being with us tonight."

Brother Beerwolf managed to crack a big smile.

"Wipe that stupid smile off your face boy," Tank demanded.

Brother Beerwolf quickly obeyed.

"Our one and only starting freshman halfback last year only to be kicked off the team a year later for conduct too time consuming to even bring up was parked last Saturday night at the main stoplight on highway 44 waiting for the light to turn green-and it did 15 times, but Brother Beerwolf didn't notice because he was passed out at the wheel. Wipe those stupid smirks off your face you goofballs," Tank slammed his stick again on the table. "Thank goodness your clever little twit brother-in-law is a local politician and attorney."

Tank stood up took his cigar out of his mouth and pointed it at the members, "Gentlemen, as of now your alumni funds have been cut off." Sighs, moans and gasps could be heard throughout the room. "Shape up, or ship out," Tank warned. "Our alumni are fed up with this freak farm. Get your act together, or I will have National shut this puppy down so quick it will make your heads spin. Do I make myself clear?"

"YES SIR!" the members screamed.

Winston jumped up and approached the general, "But sir, we need more advance notice. We have to have $4,000 dollars if we are going to have our fall General's Ball. You know how important that is to our fraternity."

The general, unperturbed, cracked a satanic smile and said, "I suggest, President Fox, that you all quit slobbering around in beer halls, and find jobs that will keep you out of trouble."

With that the General made one final warning, "Good night, Gentlemen, you have until the end of this fall semester to get your act together. I will return at your last chapter meeting of the fall semester to check your progress. If you correct the problems I addressed then your alumni financial support will continue in the spring. If you don't, you will be history."

Tank opened the heavy metal door slowly, but then slammed it hard behind him - so hard that the vibrations echoed about the chapter room like rifle fire. It was the only sound heard for awhile, for there was total silence as the chapter members sat dumbfounded and mystified.

Winston finally gained his composure, and nonchalantly motioned for Brother Beerwolf to get up. "What the hell are you waiting for Brother Beerwolf?" Winston asked giving him a mischievous wink. "Get the damn keg out of the kitchen and start passing out the cups."

"Yes sir, Brother Plato," Beerwolf hurried to the kitchen and hollered out, "Any great words of wisdom, Brother Plato?"

Winston answered immediately, "At this time, Brother Beerwolf, it is better to have four thousand beers more than you need, than four beers less than you want." Cheers and whistles roared through the room.

"We didn't elect Brother Plato Pres' for nothin," Brother Horno the Magnificent commented holding his cup of beer high in the air. Soon cups of beer were passed around like sandbags at an army front line, noted Brother Sabotage who had recently returned from three years in Vietnam as a Special Forces ranger.

Brother Pens, the chapter's treasurer stood up to address his best friend, Winston. "Mr. President, I respectfully request that the executive council meet immediately for consultation on our chapter's future plans." His worried face unfortunately didn't seem to reflect the mood of his fellow Brothers.

Winston took a large sip from his beer cup and a long drag from his newly lit cigarette, and then spoke, "Brothers, tomorrow is Friday and Blue Ridge Ski Valley in Taos is calling for us. I say road trip. Brother Billy The Kid Long will provide us with a charter bus for free, thanks to his family owning the bus line. Our suspended Brother Surf, bartends at the Blue Feather Ski Lodge. Winston paused to gloat, "I talked to him this afternoon. We can stay there for next to nothing. So?" Winston yelled, "What's your verdict?"

Cheers echoed through the room along with heavy feet stomping and cups flying through the air.

"Screw Tank, if he can't take a joke," hollered Brother Beerwolf.

"I assume that the answer is yes," Winston concluded pounding on his gavel, "meeting adjourned."

Chapter

Three

"Oh, come on, Gloria," Winston pleaded as he pulled another beer from the ice chest next to his bed. "Please, pretty please, it will be different this time, I promise." Winston fiddled nervously with the phone cord swinging it around and around like a jump rope as he talked.

"It's no use," Gloria refused to budge, "I'm not going with you tomorrow. Remember Winston, I went with you last spring break for five days, and never once did we ski. You holed up in the lounge at the ski resort the whole time."

Damn, Winston moaned to himself, *she's really not going to give in this time.* "Please, Gloria, I double promise we will ski both days," Winston again pleaded, "I give you my Kappa Kappa word of honor."

"Oh, Winston, damn your hide," Gloria sighed, "You're

a broken record. Over and over again I want to believe you only to get disappointed again and again – I feel like Charlie Brown, and besides I have better things to do than go on a weekend drunken orgy with a bunch of your A-teamin' beer buddies," Gloria stopped for a second, and waited for a reply but there was none. "I'm sorry Winston. You can always stay here and we will go horseback riding in Palo Duro Canyon – it's beautiful down there in the fall – the leaves are just now turning."

Screw the leaves, Winston thought as he lit a cigarette and sat up higher on his bed.

"Winston, hang on I will be right back."

Winston finished the last sip from his beer, crushed the can and pitched it at the small trash can across the room, hitting the wall behind it and dropping it in. "Bingo, Winston. Two points," Winston patiently waited for Gloria to return to the phone. He pulled another beer from his cooler, turned around and stared at the four foot tall aquarium that was basically his headboard.

Often at night he would sit on his bed in total darkness except for the lighted fish tank before him and reflect on the day's events, both locally and nationally. Outwardly, Winston acted the role of just another easy going, happy go lucky gent, but in reality he was much more serious about current affairs and life in general than he would let on.

He kept staring at the tropical fish as they floated effortlessly about like leaves blowing on a quiet fall day. The large striped fish that Winston nicknamed Herman would occasionally touch the tank's glass right in front of Winston as though the fish was blowing kisses at him.

Winston smiled, "Imagine, I'm getting hustled by a fish and I don't even know what sex it is."

"Winston, hello, are you there?" Gloria asked, "Are you

there?"

"Sure, my sweet, are you coming with me tomorrow?" Winston begged once again, "The whole weekend will be ruined for me if you are not there."

"That was sweet, honey," Gloria answered with tenderness in her voice, "But, Winston, you don't want me to be your girl, you want me to be your nurse."

Winston scooted up higher against the pillows, took one long sip of beer, and quickly gave himself a pep talk. *Come on, Winston, it's the fourth quarter. Time is running out and you're losing; do something!*

"Gloria, again, I give you my Kappa Kappa word of honor," Winston promised, "and I will take you skiing all day Saturday. We'll go to the back slope where the championship run, Lonesome Quail is. There will be hardly anybody around."

Winston paused to pat himself on the back. *That a boy, Brother Plato, you are on a roll.* He continued his plea, "I can just see the winter wonderland now, big snowflakes softly floating down like butterfly wings. Pine trees covered white, and deer prancing about leaving hoof trails in the snow. It will be just you and me, Gloria. What do you say, okay?" One of the few principles Winston managed to somehow learn in his salesmanship class was when you asked for the sale, always end it with an okay. As Winston remembered, studies before had proven that most customers answered an okay with an okay. Winston eagerly awaited her answer, but was careful not to speak. He who speaks first loses. Winston remembered that principle also, even though he dropped the course.

"Okay, Winston," Gloria reluctantly agreed, "But I'm going to hold you to your word. No weaseling out, I'm warning you."

Winston smiled with delight, "Don't worry, Gloria," he comforted her doubts, "We will have one hell of a good time."

"And Winston, don't get your hopes up," Gloria warned, "I will sleep in the same bed with you, but that's it."

"Oh, Gloria," Winston frowned in frustration, "It's 1969, the free love era. 'Get it while you can,' Joplin sang, 'don't turn your back on love.'"

"It won't work, Winston. Don't argue."

"Whatever you say, my sweet. See you at the Kappa House at 3 p.m. tomorrow. The bus will be waiting out front."

"Goodnight, Winston."

"Goodnight, Gloria," Winston kept the phone to his left ear after Gloria had hung up, listening to the dial tone until finally the operator recording came on. Laying the phone down, he turned sideways and stared at the fish in the lighted aquarium. "Damn it, Herman," Winston moaned, "What's it ever going to take? Before Gloria, I scored seven straight times on the first date with sorority girls."

Herman's eyes just stared at Winston, and then the beautiful blue and yellow striped fish wiggled about and quietly floated away to the other side of the tank.

The American Trailways tour bus pulled into the Kappa Kappa house's circular driveway. Billy The Kid Long, the designated driver on this junket, hopped out hollering at his Brothers and their dates who had gathered around. "What do you say, y'all? I say let's hit the trail." Loud cheers and whistles followed, as the group wasted no time in boarding the bus.

Winston approached Billy, "Thanks for the loan of your tour bus. We owe you one."

"No sweat, Sherlock," Billy stepped up on the bus and sat down at the driver's seat.

Winston asked, "What about ammo?"

"Now really, Winston, this is Billy you are talking to, remember? There's 24 of us going, so I figured two kegs, one going and one returning, and Brother Plato, I might add, this is one traveling grocery store. I got cigs, chips, pizza, Boone's Farm wine for the girls, and cards." Billy gloated, "Anything you want, I got it."

"Stupid question," Winston grinned. "We'll settle up with you when we get to Taos."

Winston checked his watch, 3:05 p.m. "Damn, where's Gloria? She is never, ever late." Winston looked around but Gloria was nowhere in sight. "Surely she didn't change her mind?"

By now, everybody had loaded the bus and restlessly waited for Winston to board.

"Come on, Brother Plato," Beerwolf hollered out his open window, "Time to haul ass."

Winston nervously checked his watch again – 3:15, he noted as his eyes searched the surrounding area for any sign of Gloria.

"WINSTON," Gloria yelled out as she appeared from the front side of the bus. "Sorry I'm late. I decided at the last minute to walk, and it took longer than I thought it would."

Cheers and clapping sounds roared from the bus inside.

"Let's get this dude on the road," Roll'em Rick directed. "We're wastin' valuable time."

"Hi, Gloria," Winston smiled. "You had me worried there for a minute." Just as the two stepped up onto the bus, they noticed a rather odd kid walking toward the bus, backpack on, carrying an 8-track player as he played his red harmonica.

Gloria, puzzled, turned to Winston, "Who is he? Surely not

one of your new pledges."

"Not hardly, Gloria," Winston answered. "I guess you haven't met Brother Music Man have you, from the pledge class of fall 1965?"

"Are you kidding me, Winston?"

"No, I'm not. This is Roger Ray, a bona fide Kappa Kappa, who at the ripe old age of eight was abandoned by his parents at a Carnegie Hall concert. No one ever heard from them again."

Winston shook his head in sympathy as he watched The Music Man approach the bus. "Later he ended up at Boys Town, right up the road from here. He flunked out of West Texas State in 1966, was drafted, and then spent a year and a half suffering in the North Vietnam P.O.W. camp before his unexplained release." Winston shook his head as Gloria watched Roger with interest.

"He was literally beaten to a pulp by two of the guards after they caught Roger humming the tune of *America the Beautiful* on his imaginary harmonica."

"Oh," was all Gloria could muster, "how dreadful."

"Bless his skinny little heart," Winston reflected, "he seldom eats, and he's the only one in our fraternity that doesn't drink. Since he re-enrolled this fall, he rarely talks to anybody, but his love for music is mind boggling. He's either blarin' songs out from his 8-track portable player, or he's playing his red harmonica or he's ear plugged into his transistor radio. But, damn, Gloria," Winston grinned with admiration, "Roger has an uncanny knack for picking the perfect song for the right occasion." Winston paused and threw his hands up in a hopeless gesture, "Our only problem is where we're going to hide him come next spring rush."

"Oh, Winston, shame on you."

Billy sounded the bus horn loudly. "Come on, Winston, the natives back here are getting restless."

"Come on, Music Man, all aboard, we're getting out of here," Winston beckoned. "Make it 25, Billy, we have a new passenger."

"Call me Roger," was all the pale thin kid would say as he boarded the tour bus.

A large cheering ovation blared out the bus windows from the passengers inside.

"Forward, ho," roared Brother Rodeo Cool, as wild yells and whistles encored the order, so loud that Gloria covered her ears to block out the noise.

An hour and fifteen minutes later the single bus caravan approached the New Mexico border.

"Finally," Billy sighed, "no more mesquite bushes, playa lakes, and flat farmland." Billy grinned as he remembered flying over this flat land only a month before. "Reminds me of a huge checkerboard of wheat and corn squares."

Just a short distance ahead, Billy could see the landscape changing around them. Soon mesas and tall pine trees would dot the flat country side. This changing landscape meant that towering mountain ranges would soon appear in the distance, and this view would make the five and a half hour journey a lot less tedious.

"Pizza, anyone?" Brother Dancin' Beerwolf asked pulling five large to go boxes from a wrapped container.

Two hours later, the passengers inside the bus were up to their usual form. The first keg was half way to drained, empty pizza boxes and potato chip bags were strung down the aisle. They passed the time by singing fraternity songs and telling the usual, often repeated, stories about each other. Most of the girls, tired of the same ol', same ol' gathered in the back.

Gloria, sitting on the window side next to Winston gazed out at the ever changing terrain, admiring the beautiful sunset that had emerged in the western sky. She quietly watched the sun's final descent into the soft gray clouds that hovered above the snow capped mountains. Then her attention turned back to the rowdy crowd's annoying behavior behind them. "Winston, you promised me."

"Cool your jets, my sweet, we are partying tonight, but tomorrow will be all yours." Winston sat up, stretched and walked down the aisle for a refill. As he passed, shouts of "What's happening, Brother Plato," and high fives reached out slapping Winston's outstretched arms as he fought his way to the back.

"Hey dudes, the Prez is coming our way," Roll'em Rick pointed. Winston filled his cup and returned to his seat.

The entire time they had been on the road, the Music Man sat quietly alone in the very back row meticulously tinkering with wires and speakers.

Gloria whispered in Winston's ear, "What's Roger doing back there?"

"It is my guess that we are about to hear a great sound system for the remainder of the trip," Winston abruptly stood up and called out to Roger. "Hey, Music Man, got it working yet?"

Roger nodded his head almost without notice.

"What's your pleasure?" Winston asked.

Moments later Steppenwolf's *Born to be Wild* blasted out from the two large speakers next to Roger.

The Kappas and their dates yelled their approval as they all started singing "Headin' out on the highway, looking for adventure…"

"Way to go Music Man," Brother Spoon cheered.

Thirty minutes later the tour bus drove into the picturesque small town of Springer, located in the foothills of the northern New Mexico mountain ranges.

"Yea, Springer," Brother Horne the Magnificent yelled, "we're nearly there."

"All right, Music Man, what's our next song?" Brother Sgt. T. asked. "How about one from the Beatles?"

"Call me Roger," he mumbled in a low voice, "call me Roger," and then he turned and switched 8-tracks. A familiar song known to them all soon followed, "What would you do if I sang out of tune…"

"Perfecto, Roger," Winston said, "it can't get any better than *With A Little Help From My Friends*." The passengers again started singing the lyrics, this time so loud that the tape could barely be heard.

By now, the bright red sun had slowly disappeared behind the mountains ahead.

Winston put his arm around Gloria pointing out the window at the brilliant red sky. "Isn't this beautiful country?" Winston asked. "No wonder the native Indians call this state 'The Land of Enchantment.' Gloria, we are in luck," Winston teased.

"Why is that?"

"Starting sometime after midnight, they are predicting eight inches of new snow will fall by tomorrow afternoon."

Billy the Kid grabbed the microphone beside him and announced out loud, "All right fellow Kappas, time to settle down. We are now about an hour and a half away, and we have lots of partying ahead of us. I say nap time, children."

Groans, boos and grunts of disappointment answered Billy's request with obvious discontent. After awhile the restless group had settled down. The singing, dancing and joke telling had stopped. A melancholy mood finally settled in as the protests grew increasingly quieter. The sky above them darkened, only bright stars could be seen overlooking this pitch black wilderness of no man's land. The stars shined so bright and appeared so close that Gloria said, "I could almost grab one of them with my hand."

"All right, Roger, set the mood," Brother Pens requested. Seconds later with the volume softly lowered and the lyrics from a great Doors song sounded out. "Riders in the sky…"

Winston smiled his approval and then kissed Gloria on her right cheek as she was now fast asleep, resting her head on a pillow against the window.

Winston tiptoed to the back, refilled his beer cup, and carefully returned to the front of the bus. Leaning against the tall rail with his right foot standing on the second step, he smiled at Billy as they zoomed along the blacktop, "Well, what do you think, pal? Is this great or what?"

Billy just nodded his head, but then whispered, "But, Brother Plato, what are we going to do when we return?"

"No bad vibes," Winston lectured, who by his own admission was part ostrich, "No bad vibes. As Scarlett O'Hara would say, I will think about that tomorrow."

Winston's mood soured a little and he lit up a cigarette as he stared at the sleeping passengers in the bus. His serious nature took control as he sized up several of his long time Kappa friends.

On the second row directly in front of him was Dancin' Beerwolf - his real and only name. Beerwolf was a full blooded Cheyenne Indian who loved to dress the part wearing turquoise jewelry and Taos western outfits. When he wasn't carousing and honky tonking the Amarillo bar scenes, he was a damn good watercolor artist and sculptor.

"One of the best I have ever seen," observed Rick Wallace,

head of the Art Department at WTSU. But his work was few and far between. He had definite Indian features and looked like a young Sitting Bull. Jet black hair, hook nose, strong character lines below his brown eyes and heavy for his 5'10" frame. Winston would swear the man never slept. He was everywhere - he knew everyone and was loved by them all. In his own way, Beerwolf was the most valuable asset to the fraternity. He could get any project accomplished, whether it was finding totally nude strippers for a rush party, or hiring a great band for the Kappa dances, he could pull it off.

Beerwolf loved to dance, dance, dance. Whether it was doing his Cheyenne war dance at the Spring Stock Rodeo, or the two step at the western clubs, particularly at the Midnight Corral, or just rocking out at the various Amarillo nightclubs, it didn't matter, when the music started playing Dancin' Beerwolf would instinctively start to shuffle his feet.

As Brother Roll'em Rick would say it best, "Man, the dude looks like a rooster on acid."

Winston smiled at that thought, yawned, and turned his attention to Billy, "You awake?"

"Of course," Billy answered, "just visualizing how I'm going to beat Earl the Pearl when I take his money next Tuesday on the golf course."

"Always thinking, aren't you, Billy?" Winston said smiling.

"Is there any other way, Brother Plato?" Billy's confidence was impressive.

In the seat across the aisle from Brother Beerwolf, lay a motionless John, Brother Sgt. T. Pepper and his older in appearance, oriental girlfriend. Winston grinned because he couldn't tell whether he was asleep or not because of John's dark round rimmed sunglasses.

What an enigma. Winston thought. John had been an honor roll student his first three years at WTSU before joining the Navy seals in1967. He returned after one and a half years of heavy action in Vietnam, almost mortally wounded. John was never the same afterward. He had little desire to study and instead focused his attention to guitar playing, song writing, and singing.

John literally became mesmerized by the Beatles, and in particular, idolized John Lennon. Every day he would transform himself into Lennon's character, wearing a fatigue jacket like the one he had on tonight, with an Irish wool hat - everything vintage Lennon, including his round rimmed glasses, his long brown straight hair and his constant habit of giving people around him the peace sign.

Winston shook his head and smiled. After a few drinks, not only would Sgt. T. recite Lennon's song lyrics, he actually believed they were his own. His look-alike Lennon appearance and manner sometimes would be so convincing that on occasions he would be mobbed by screaming teenage girls at sporting events and movie theaters who sought his autograph.

Winston glanced out the windshield at pitch darkness. "How much longer, Kid?"

"Oh, maybe an hour or so."

"Can I get you anything?"

"Just a straighter pool cue, Brother Plato."

Winston smiled, "Always hustlin' aren't you Kid? How much did you take in bookin' last weekend's football games?"

"Little over $200."

Winston nodded, *Not bad for a weekend.* He turned his attention back to the sleeping passengers. Behind Sgt. T., and sitting by himself taking up both seats, was Troy, Brother

Sabotage, Tyson. Smashed in nose and bulldog appearance, Troy was the fraternity's work of art. Son of the most decorated officer in the Korean conflict - and one mean son of a bitch. Twenty inch neck, huge ox-like shoulders and still he maintained a 34" waist. Winston cracked a smirk as he recalled that not so long ago Troy attempted to purchase a navy blazer in the local clothing store, but the salesman just shook his head and walked away.

Troy's story was similar to Sgt. T.'s, and his own, but different too. Troy left WTSU in the summer of 1965 to serve in the Marines. He served three straight years in special forces deep in the Vietnam jungles and was wounded four times before fate smiled and allowed him to return to the states and back to West Texas State. Before Troy joined the Marines, he was considered the finest athlete ever to enroll in the university. Plus he was an absolute genius with an I.Q. of 170 plus. Troy could do anything and his mechanical ingenuity was second to none. He was a brilliant electrician, brilliant engineer, and could operate any machine. With his service he had also become a top munitions expert.

As with most of the young men that served in Vietnam, war left bitter scars that never healed. Troy rarely laughed or even smiled for that matter. He appeared unhappy and his eyes gave you the chilling conclusion that they wanted to blow something up, but did not know yet exactly what that would be.

Winston put out his cigarette on the step and tiptoed quietly down the aisle, carefully dodging full beer cups, potato chip bags, and dangling arms, but managed to make his way to the keg. Winston waved to Roger in the back row. He was wide awake, earplugs in, as he quietly listened to his radio. Roger did not wave back, instead just raised his index finger of his left hand. Winston tiptoed back through the trash to the front of the bus.

Billy took his hands from the wheel, and quietly clapped several times. He silently congratulated Winston's mission impossible.

Winston smiled, "Thanks, Billy, for the loan of your tour bus. We needed a break."

"No problem, Brother Plato, but you know I don't do anything for free."

"I know, Kid," Winston shrugged, unconcerned.

"After we all divvy up to pay for all of this, I should clear about $200,and I figure that's a bargain, considering I provided the transportation, gas and 12 hours of driving."

"I agree," Winston answered, "a bargain the way I see it." Winston inhaled on another cigarette and studied his new subject, and his favorite gambling golf partner, Brother Billy The Kid Long.

At least Billy had a hell of a lot going for him, more so than the rest of the motley Kappa crew. Billy was what you might call a 'connector'. He was the middle man or go between for any transaction imaginable that would produce a profit. He came across as a cute kid with a baby face and looked barely 17. It was probably pretty scary for other drivers to see what looked like a little kid wielding this massive bus hurtling down the highway. But a young appearance was just that – an appearance. Behind that baby face was one shrewd calculating mastermind. Billy was a scratch golfer, one hell of a pot limit poker player, and a very competent pool shooter.

Billy also doubled as a part time bookie and would bet on anything if the odds favored him, while his attitude and style stayed cool as a cucumber. He never seemed to show any sign of weakness or let on that anything unnerved him. It was a joke between them that Winston would always ask, "Been watchin' to many Steve McQueen movies lately haven't you?" Billy's own motto was 'Never let them see you sweat'. His one claim to fame which took place sometime in the summer of 1968, was that he beat world champion poker player Amarillo Slim in a heads up $1,000 Texas Hold 'em freeze out poker game that lasted nineteen hours straight. That said a lot for his determination and stamina.

"Winston what's spinnin' around in that Plato mind of yours?" Billy asked. "Why so serious, are you getting a buzz?"

Winston let out a weak chuckle, "No, Billy just trying to review the troops before the big battle ahead."

"What the hell are you talking about?"

"Never mind, Kid, we will all know sooner than we want to know." Winston stood up and stretched, "I'm crashing for an hour or so, can you handle this ship without a copilot?"

"Rest up, Winston, the night has just begun."

Winston sat down in the seat beside Gloria, laid his head gently on her shoulder, and fell quietly asleep.

Except for Roger who had just put on a Moody Blues tape, Billy was the only person that was still awake, or at least he far could tell, as he drove slowly through the historic section of Taos. He directed the bus through the narrow streets toward the ski area not far ahead. Billy checked the southwest flavor of the scenery out as he turned the bus onto the narrow road that led up to the ski area. *Just a typical western outpost, except for this one is a little more famous, why I don't know*, Billy thought. *Nothing here but hippies, native Indians, artists, and adobe structures of one design or another.*

Billy grabbed the small black microphone, "All right, Brother Kappa Kappas," he announced loudly over the P.A. "We are almost there. Blue Feather Ski Lodge is not far away." Billy guided the bus around the sharp curve ahead as they made their way up the steep, winding mountain road. Tall thick forests of mostly pine and aspen trees dotted the landscape along their way, and much to their surprise, large soft snowflakes fell so thick that Billy could barely see through his windshield, no matter how fast the wipers went or how hot the defroster blew. Billy's vision was limited and to compensate for this winter distraction, he continued to slow his speed - sometimes almost to a crawl.

"Damn, what is it going to take?" He moaned tired from the long drive, "Another hour to go a measly five miles?"

"Wake up, Gloria," Winston urged, "look out the window. It's a winter wonderland."

"All right, Brothers," Billy again announced, "looks like Custer's last stand back there." Billy slowly negotiated the sharp treacherous turn just ahead. Fearing ice on the road, he slowed his speed to almost a standstill.

"Brother Music Man," Billy requested, "wake these deadbeats up."

Roger, showing no emotion, put in a new 8-track tape and turned the volume up as loud as it would go. Soon the sound of the Rolling Stones blared out, "Start me up, start me up, I'll never stop…"

Dancin' Beerwolf, along with his cute red-headed girlfriend, Heidi, jumped up and started dancing in the aisles. "It's party time, Kappas," he urged, "get ready, get ready to go."

Billy guided the bus up the last of the narrow windy road. The tension on his face was starting to show. "Damn it, this snow is so thick I can hardly see."

Winston hearing a heightened level of concern in Billy's voice, walked up to the front of the bus, "How we doin' Kid?"

"Brother Plato, I think one more turn and we're there."

Five minutes later the heavily snow packed bus approached

the historic Blue Feather Ski Lodge, and finally the tedious journey had reached its destination. The tour bus slowly entered the front parking area. The lodge was truly a masterpiece. Built in the late 1950's, this famous ski lodge stood proudly like a magnificent European cathedral. It's rock and wood structure seemed to dangle like an eagle's nest off the mountain side as it overlooked the deep valley below.

"Where's the bar?" Brother Horno the Magnificent asked as the entourage hurried into the spacious lounge area. A cathedral ceiling extended high above them, and wagon wheel chandeliers brightly lit, hung from the solid wood beams. Thick cedar walls encircled the room decorated with southwest landscape paintings and lithographs displaying western Indian culture. Everywhere you turned you could see mounted trophies of fish, bison heads, elk, long horn sheep - you name it it was there. Three large stone fireplaces lit the room with an orange and reddish glow. Two grizzly bears mounted in their standing attack positions bookended the largest fireplace, their teeth snarling and claws reaching to the point they looked a little too real.

"This hairy dude is after my ass," Roll 'em Rick blurted, backing quickly away.

"Just statues, Rick." Rodeo Cool guided Rick toward the circular bar just ahead.

"Wow, could have fooled me," Rick removed his black leather jacket. "This dude lodge reminds me of a backdrop for one of them Wayne westerns."

"A western English castle is my take," Brother Pens surmised, "sure would hate to pay the utility bills." To their left was a bandstand and dance floor, and to their right on the north wall was a solid plate glass window that covered almost the entire wall. One could look out and see the picturesque ski runs below glistening with new fallen snow.

The group approached the old circular mahogany bar, admiring the solid brass top and brass foot rails. The owners of the lodge found this gem in an old mining town in Montana, years back, and literally had the 100 year old antique, crated and shipped to the lodge for reassembly.

"Hey, guys," Kappa Brother Ronnie Surf Hudson came out from the store room behind the bar, "glad to see you made it." Surf was a tall good looking lad, who kept an almost eternal smile on his face, which showed his large front teeth that had a noticeable gap. His hair was blond and very short for 1960's standards, and he had a cowlick at the front of his part that he constantly would brush down with his hands, but the effort was hopeless.

"First round is on the house," Surf poured draft beers as fast as he could. "Look who's sitting at my brass bar?" Surf smiled as he took in his new patrons. "All my favorite Brothers - Brother Plato, Brother Spoon, Brother Beerwolf, Brother Sgt. T., Brother Sabotage, Brother Roll 'em, Brother Kid, and the world famous Brother Horno the Magnificent." Surf laughed, "It can't get any cooler than this."

The rest of the gathering scattered about as they admired the decor of the lodge's interior. Gloria was the only girl that joined the gang at the bar.

"And I might add," Surf smiled as he reached across the bar to kiss Gloria on the right cheek. "What the hell are you doing here with these renegades?"

"Just the usual babysitting duties that one would expect to encounter, when I stupidly agreed to go."

Winston grinned, but didn't clarify. "The rest of us know why, but tell Brother Sabotage why you are here, and not back in school. I don't think he's heard your story."

Surf hesitated for a moment, and then said, "Last spring our wonderful Dean of Women, Agnes Peabody, who also was the Eta Zeta's faculty advisor, talked my fiancée into breaking off our engagement, because in Agnes' own words, "Jamie don't lower yourself to this Kappa loser, you can do so much better." Surf frowned and turned away for a second, and then continued with his story, his broad smile covered up his still raw emotions. "So during my older Brother Larry's honor society luncheon that Agnes was guest speaker, I dressed up as his date and we sat down on the very front row." Surf grinned and bounced his brows. "I have to say I looked pretty damn sexy in my red mini dress and newly shaved long legs, blond wig and all."

Brother Horno the Magnificent let out a loud wolf whistle.

"Down boy, Brother Horno," Winston said.

"Anyway," Surf continued, "as our lovely Dean of Women was addressing the honor students, I constantly crossed and uncrossed my legs wearing no panties or panty hose. I flashed a bit of 'hose' if you know what I mean. She turned ghost white and fainted clean away. Her head knocked the microphone off the podium as she crashed right behind it. Luckily she wasn't hurt."

"Go on," Winston urged.

"I quietly slipped away undetected, but one of the Zeta girls recognized me. She should have, the little bitch, since I had dated her the year before. Didn't know she was there. Anyway after the dust settled, I was indefinitely suspended for God knows how long," Surf paused to sip on a newly poured soda.

"How long?" Kid asked concerned.

"Oh, hell, who knows," Surf replied shaking his head. "The letter said the suspension would be of a permanent nature, whatever the hell that means. Another beer anyone?"

"So what are you going to do now?" Gloria asked.

"I'll get my New Mexico residency pretty soon, so I think I will enroll at the University in Albuquerque."

"Man, what a bummer," Roll'em moaned.

"Relax Brothers," Surf encouraged, "pretty soon the best band in New Mexico, none other than Mr. Soul and The Sundancers themselves will start playing. So I suggest you spread out, sit by the fireplaces, and have a few appetizers, because the night is about to begin." Loud cheers followed Surf's announcement.

Winston and Gloria left the bar and sat down at the table next to the largest roaring fireplace. "Damn that pinion wood smells good," Winston said.

Gloria had struck up a conversation with Beerwolf's date, Heidi, who had sat down beside her.

"Where's Beerwolf?" Winston asked Heidi.

"Who knows and who cares?" Heidi replied sarcastically, "Probably putting on his dancing war paint for all I know."

Winston scooted his chair away from the table, lit a cigarette and stared almost trance-like into the roaring flames, and then his eyes darted back and forth as he observed his fellow Brothers. Roll 'em Rick Hopper seemed determined to have a good time this weekend. Winston paused as he took a deep drag from his cigarette and blew the smoke into the fireplace. Rick was the clean cut farm boy type from a small cotton growing town of 800 people but that was before he saw the movie *Easy Rider* 93 times and counting. Overnight he became West Texas State's first real hippie. He sported the Fu Manchu beard, extremely long hair and he could always be seen wearing dark sunglasses even indoors. He wore his black leather jacket, even when he wasn't riding his souped up Harley.

Everybody Rick ever met was named 'Dude'. He was the Kappa's cool cat daddy, who wore his tight jeans so high up, that some of the girls would turn their heads away when he strutted through the student union building while others wondered why his voice didn't squeak. Always getting high on something, he was the alumni's biggest nightmare. The chapter would hide him when the Kappa Kappa National Commander paid a visit.

During rush, the fraternity chipped in expense money so he could take a bike trip to Taos. He was definitely not what Tank had in mind as far as the ideal Kappa Kappa.

Winston turned to Gloria, "Need anything?"

"No thank you," she gave a little smile and continued her conversation with Heidi.

Sitting next to Roll'em Rick, was none other than Charlie The Spoon Luna. Winston chugged down the remainder of his beer. Pouring another one from the pitcher Surf left on the end table, he thought about Charlie, the classic trust fund baby. Unfortunately, Charlie was typical of their kind and didn't have a real grasp on how hard life could be. Winston saw the wealthy like a bunch of poodles that had been inbred for so long they literally had their brains fucked out. Charlie wasn't all that bad, he was quiet, shy, and good lookin' with his curly blonde hair and blue eyes would have got him some tail even without the trust fund although that sure helped. He was also surprisingly intelligent and even when he was blitzed, could carry on an intense conversation about anything.

Always in a perpetual good mood, Charlie would rarely attend his classes – another problem that was plaguing the Kappas. At night, particularly when there was a full moon out, Charlie would come alive though he was rarely seen in the Kappa House after 10 p.m. Some of the Brothers had sworn that they woke in the night after hearing bone chilling howls corning from Charlie's room, but no one would ever see him and no one knew where he would go at night, and no one even wanted to know.

Next to Charlie sat Brother Horno the Magnificent Winston smiled, Horno had been a basket case from his freshman year on. He was probably the best looking and sexiest guy on campus with a great sense of humor and personality to spare. Horno loved to party, and spent most of his nights hanging out at Barnaby's Pub in Amarillo. Somehow he would manage to drive back to Palo Duro and spend the rest of the night calling up old girlfriends, begging them to come over. Sometimes in desperation he would go to their apartments or rent houses and bang on their doors pleading to be let in. He was great to have around at rush parties, but other than that, didn't have much to offer the fraternity but trouble. One good result occurred from all his late night escapades was that security in the town increased, more doors were locked at night, even windows in the hot summer months were locked and tightly shut. Horno was a legend. He possessed more sex driven hormones than a wild hyena in heat.

Winston stared at Horno's seating companion, Rodeo Cool, whose real name no one could remember. After all, this was Rodeo Cool's ninth straight year at West Texas State – with no army careers in between. He was one of the greatest, if not the best, bull riders in all of the west. Winston paused and grinned at his unusual appearance. He was a walking 6'4" monster, with a huge handlebar mustache that grew way past trimming stage, the left side stained brownish black from spittin' chewin' tobacco on any plant or corner he could find, and the right side stained Red River red from eatin' too much of his favorite beef stew. In short he looked like a really tall Yosemite Sam.

From 1965 through 1968, Rodeo Cool was the world champion bull rider. Then things changed, when he won a trip to Switzerland in the summer of 1968. In Europe, he met a sweet little maiden named Gretchen, goldilocks and all, who taught Rodeo how to yodel. From that day forward, Rodeo Cool's life took a different direction. They both returned back to the states and lived together as they both enrolled at West Texas State. Rodeo Cool retired from the bull riding scene, devoted his life to Gretchen, and they both could be seen dancing about, and constantly yodeling.

"Man, these two sound like they belong in a dog pound," Roll'em Rick said. "I hate to see someone go downhill as quick as he did."

Winston smiled at that thought giving Rodeo Cool's appearance one last glance. What a character - huge bloodshot eyes with a nose to match, and a beer belly that would knock you over. At least Cool and Gretchen were happy together.

"Winston, you okay?" Gloria asked as she walked over to Winston, putting her arm around him.

"Just contemplating, my love, just contemplating," Winston answered in a low key voice. "Maybe Tank was right when he summed up our chapter, maybe our members are starting to look a little scary."

"Come on, Winston, now's not the time for this."

"An apt observation, my dear. From now on I will focus my complete attention to this voluptuous, gorgeous princess that is now beside me."

"Good try, Winston, but it's not going to get you anywhere."

A voice interrupted them, "Good evening lads, my name is Mr. Soul, and behind me is my great band, The Sundancers."

Loud screaming cheers erupted from the audience that had gathered in the bar. As usual, Brother Dancin' Beerwolf stood up and started doing an Indian dance, slapping his open hand against his mouth.

"Sit down, dude," Roll em' Rick instructed. "Man, the music hasn't even started yet."

The distinguished looking black man behind the mike with his short curly gray hair spoke again, "Are you white boys ready to party or do you even know how?"

Screams of enthusiasm greeted his question.

Six songs later, Winston approached the circular bar, motioning to Surf to pour him another beer. "You weren't kidding were you, Surf," Winston pointed out, "this is one hell of a band."

Surf just smiled as he poured Winston a full draft beer.

"The best band I have ever heard. You need to figure out a way to get them to play for the General's Ball this November," Surf stopped and took a hard sad look at Winston. "So damn glad to see you all, you don't know how much I miss it."

"All right, are we having fun yet?" Mr. Soul asked.

The Brothers, along with the gathering locals, yelled and whistled their appreciation.

"And now I have a surprise for you with our next song, especially played for the pretty lady over there sitting next to the fire." Mr. Soul pointed directly at Gloria, "Would this cute couple please dance a solo for Mr. Soul?"

Again whoops and hollers erupted in the crowd.

The lyrics to the popular song *Gloria* began to play, "I'm going to tell you about my baby... she's going to make me feel all right, and her name is G-l-o-r-i-a-a-a." For the next minute or two Winston and Gloria solo danced on the dance floor as their friends clapped to the beat with excitement.

"Gloria," Winston whispered into her ear as they danced. "Will you marry me?"

"Oh, Winston, damn you, you gotta tell me you love me

first."

They continued dancing until the song ended. Winston gently kissed Gloria on the lips, held her hand and started to guide her off the dance floor, but his attention shifted toward the lone clapping sound that was coming from the front entrance, "Bravo, Bravo." The man shouted clapping his hands as he and several others behind him walked past the large doorway.

"Can you believe it, Gloria?" Winston asked in amazement. "We can't seem to get far enough away without running into Michael Gentile and that little turncoat Laura Love." Winston shook his head and spoke to the unwelcome pair, "So nice to see stallion breath and our last year's Kappa sweetheart again."

"Hey, Winston," Michael blurted out as he approached the bar ordering Surf to fix a scotch on the rocks for him. "Can't believe you are still awake, figured you would be passed out by now." The group that had followed him all laughed their approval.

Winston, showing no sign of emotion, slowly sauntered up to Michael and stared into his eyes for a moment before finally answering. Imitating Humphrey Bogart's voice with perfection and mannerism, he answered, "Of all the gin joints in all of the towns in all of the world, you had to come into mine."

"The word's out all ready, Winston," Michael smirked in delight. "Did Tank pay you a little visit recently?"

Surf handed Winston a freshly poured draw, "Sorry, Brother Plato, I have no control over who the patrons are."

"No sweat, Surf," Winston offered as he walked away. "Maybe the Bronx Stallion will find time to build a snowman." Then turning back toward Michael he said, "But that will be a first for you, Michael - an actual white snowman with no black factory soot all over it."

Michael cocked his head with his usual smirk but did not reply.

Mr. Soul, watching the confrontation before him, quickly decided to loosen the audience up with his favorite song of the 1960's. Soon the lyrics to a Rolling Stones classic blasted away, "I can't get no satisfaction, I can't get no satisfaction, and I try, and I try, I can't get no..."

Winston turned, holding Gloria's hand, and headed back for their table. He muttered in a low voice, "We drive 300 miles to get away from these jokers and they show up out of nowhere."

Gloria put her arm around Winston, offering soft words of encouragement, "Don't let them get to you."

"You're right, my dear," He said. "You're always right. I will drop it."

The table's attention turned toward Michael and Laura as they calmly approached Mr. Soul. Michael stopped and whispered into Mr. Soul's right ear.

"Hey dude," Roll'em hollered out, "these cats don't know jack shit about opera."

"Hey, Michael," Brother Spoon joined in, "asking directions for the nearest ferry?" The Kappa entourage roared their approval. Mr. Soul, ignoring the catcalls, approached the microphone.

"All right, my audience, Mr. Soul knows all types of music because I am the K-i-n-g as you will soon learn as the night progresses, got that honky boys?" The mostly native Indian band behind him clapped their hands as they smiled and laughed. Mr. Soul continued, "By special request I'm going to play a new song that very few of our radio disc jockeys throughout the country have had the pleasure of hearing, but gentlemen and pretty ladies, it is the hottest dance number in the New York discotheques." Mr. Soul stopped, as he pointed his finger at the mostly puzzled audience, "And sooner or later this new wave of dancing music will sweep the country." The audience before him remained quiet and curious. Mr. Soul then turned to one of his band members, snapping his fingers. Seconds later, bright blue and yellow strobe lights darted across the dance floor, bouncing off the walls. Michael guided Laura to the middle of the dance floor, as they both awaited the beginning of the song.

Winston and Gloria sat quietly watching the action with amused curiosity.

Brother Horno, by now a bit tipsy to say the least, hollered out at the couple, "Hey, Fred Astaire, show us your stuff."

Cheers and whistles from the Kappa section followed. Mr. Soul frowned with displeasure at the rowdy behavior, and pleaded for silence. Then shouted a one, and a two, and a three.

Michael and Laura started dancin' to the new disco sound with moves and gyrations that nobody in the southwest had seen before. They twisted and turned and twirled their bodies around with professional grace and posture, Michael in perfect timing to every beat of the song *Stayin' Alive* that Mr. Soul was playing, jerked his hips side to side, and with his left arm on his stomach would extend his right arm in the air. Whether you liked their performance or not, they were certainly an impressive couple that had to have practiced this routine over and over again. Even some of the Kappas couldn't resist clapping.

"Who is this dude?" Roll'em Rick asked with contempt in his voice. "Looks like a fuckin' bullfighter on acid, man."

Winston, slightly annoyed by Gloria's obvious pleasure of the dance routine, said, "Can you believe this guy? Who the hell does he think he is, Elvis?" Winston shook his head in disbelief, "Christ, Gloria, look at that three piece polyester white suit he's wearing, and that God awful black opened collar shirt-and those goofy high heel shoes." Winston just shook his head again. Gloria, ignoring the remarks, watched the dance routine with unquestionable interest. The two continued their solo performance, egged on by cheers and whistles even from the Kappa section. The music was so good and so inviting, it literally mesmerized the onlookers as they watched the couple pull off every dance move and gesture possible. More twists, more twirls, more swirls than any fraternity party had ever seen before. The two finished their solo act by simultaneously doing the splits, and then rising together to throw their arms high into the air. The audience roared their approval, as several of them stood up to applaud Michael and Laura's performance. Mr. Soul ended the song by extending a bow to the couple.

"You have to admit, whether you like 'em or not," Manse conceded, "whatever they did out there, was darn good, don't you think, Brother Rick?"

"Oh, screw 'em," Roll'em mumbled out as he wiped the spilled beer off his black Harley leather jacket, "so the dudes are dancin' pricks. So what? My mother can dance to."

Michael put his arms around Laura, kissing her softly on the lips, and then threw his thumb up to the band, as he nonchalantly strutted over to Winston's table.

"Hey, Winston," Michael gloated, wiping the perspiration from his brow, "We kinda kicked your little dance routine in the dirt, eh?" Michael smirked as he put his hand on his cocked hip. "Come by sometime, and I will give you a dance lesson."

Winston smiled, but made sure that Michael's ribbing didn't bother him. "My suggestion, Michael, is that you don't get that rubber suit that you are wearing, too close to the fire or we will all go up in flames."

"Funny, funny, aren't you farm boy?" Michael retorted.

"So cocky even when your ship is nearly vertical." Michael smirked, took Laura's hand, and strutted away, throwing one final verbal jab, "Can you spell the word 'Titanic'? Or have you ever made it through a history class?"

Winston smiled and waved goodbye, "I think I would rather be on the Titanic right now, than next to that sweat suit you are wearing."

Mr. Soul grabbed the microphone, "Say, all you honkys out there," he laughed in a teasing spirit, "were they not good?"

A chorus of cheers followed that was soon drowned out by loud boos and jeers coming from the Kappa section of the room. "All right, gentlemen," Mr. Soul continued, "to keep you limber and sober, we are gonna start jiving to a little Caribbean limbo music. The tall dark Indian trumpet player stepped down from the bandstand, setting up the long bamboo limbo stick on two wooden sets.

"What the hell?" Sgt. T. asked.

"Haven't you heard the song *Limbo Rock* before?" Roger spoke up for the first time since they left on the trip, and then he sang a few lyrics out loud, "Jack be nimble, Jack be quick, Jacked jumped over the candlestick."

"Can you believe it?" Brother Sabotage explained, "Roger actually removing his earplugs and talking?"

"Now I'm catchin' on," Dancin' Beerwolf answered, "but I gotta be careful, I might spill my beer."

"All right all you frat rats out there and you pretty ladies," Mr. Soul announced motioning them to get up. "Time to line up."

"Come on, Brothers," Charlie The Spoon encouraged, "This will be fun."

Led by a smiling Dancin' Beerwolf, several Brothers and their dates lined up. Mr. Soul wasn't satisfied with the participation. Turning his attention toward Michael and his gathering, he ordered, "What's the matter with you boys, are you afraid?"

"Come on, Deltas, let's show 'em up," Michael instructed.

"These dudes are nuts," commented Roll'em' Rick, "I wouldn't do that even on my Harley." Brother Sabotage, along with Sgt. T. also remained seated at their table.

For the next several minutes the band blared out the limbo beat, as the participants limboed underneath, going around and around again as the trumpet player lowered the bamboo stick a notch each time.

Winston who also remained seated turned to Gloria. "Why aren't you up there?"

"In my mini-dress?" Gloria answered. "I think I will pass, thank you."

Winston lit a cigarette as he watched the line of participants slowly dwindle in size, as the bamboo stick was lowered, again and again. The first person eliminated was, of course, Rodeo Cool, who on his first try fell backwards hitting his head on the dance floor. He lay there for a few seconds, his red shirt open in the front from two missing buttons, as he coughed heavily.

"Damn chew," Rodeo mumbled as his Brothers helped him get up. Second person eliminated, or should we say disqualified, was Charlie The Spoon Luna, who on his first try took a head first dive, sliding underneath the limbo stick. "Safe!" Charlie hollered out as he jumped up and brushed off the dust on his jeans.

"Out," Mr. Soul pointed at Charlie, waving him off the dance floor.

Third person eliminated was poor ol' Dancin' Beerwolf who on his fifth try under the limbo stick, fell sideways, spilling the glass of beer that he was carrying all down his tan leather fringed shirt. "Please," he begged Mr. Soul, "Please give me one more chance." Beerwolf looked sadly at Mr. Soul.

"Off!" Mr. Soul directed, motioning Beerwolf to leave. The music continued, as the bamboo stick was lowered. "Jack be nimble, Jack be quick…"

Kappa Brother Jumpin Jack Flash, knowing that the stick's new height was too low for him to limbo under, took a running leap, scissoring sideways over the stick.

"Off!" Mr. Soul ordered, shaking his head hopelessly, "This ain't no track meet."

By now only Michael, Heidi, and one other girl were left. On the next go around the pretty tall blond, her back arched back so far, it was almost painful to watch didn't make it. Her boobs knocked the stick over.

Heidi quickly followed, falling back on the floor, her blue miniskirt rose up over her waist. Catcalls and whistles followed.

"Looks like we got a winner," Mr. Soul stepped down to congratulate Michael.

"Not yet, Mr. Soul, let's give Winston Fox a chance to beat me."

Turning toward Winston he said, "How about it Plato, I say $50 bucks to the winner." Michael loved it, the smirk glowed on his face, as he muttered under his breath, "He ain't got a chance, no way he could limbo under the stick - it's barely two feet high."

Winston sat calmly without answering, as he listened to the Deltas razz 'em.

"What are you going to do?" Gloria asked, "He's trying to make a fool out of you."

Winston took a drag from his cigarette, and blew it out. "You know, Gloria, the limbo originated in the West Indies. It was an acrobatic dance that only men participated in."

"How did you know that?" She asked.

"I practiced this crap in high school in a Caribbean school play, over and over again until I could hardly walk." Winston smiled as he sipped on his beer and then bragged, "Hell, I got so damn good, I could beat anybody."

"Can you beat, Michael?"

"I don't know, that was a long ways back."

"Well," Michael taunted, "one last chance, chicken."

"Damn him, he's tryin' to embarrass our Pres.," Sgt. T. moaned.

"You're on, stallion breath, I could use a little beer money."

Winston stood up, removed his socks and shoes, turned to Gloria and gave his assessment of the situation. "He's in great shape, thin and strong, but I can beat this guy. When the limbo stick is this low it takes more technique and expertise than muscles. And besides those bird legs of his won't stand up to the pressure."

"Good luck, Winston."

Winston sauntered up to the dance floor. The Kappas let out loud rebel yells and hoots.

"Beat that prick," Brother Sabotage yelled out, as he had to be restrained by his Brothers from going after him.

"Get him, Michael!" Laura Love screamed as loud as she could. The Deltas followed the outcry with loud, cheering support for Michael.

Mr. Soul smiled at the two in front of him, "Well, look what we have here. We got us a honky duel." Mr. Soul snapped his fingers, motioning for the stick to be lowered a notch. "Let's start limbo rockin."

Winston was first. "Well, here goes," he whispered to himself, as he reviewed quickly what he had learned years back. The Kappas and their dates gathered around the dance floor on the north side, cheering and stomping their feet. On the other side was Michael's group as they cheered and hollered also, but they were no match compared to the Kappa cheering section.

"Jack be nimble, Jack be…" Winston started forward inching toward the bamboo stick that was at his eye level, at the same time he arched his back, as far as he could without losing his balance. *It's all in the legs.* Winston coached himself, *it's all in the legs.* Slowly he scooted his feet forward, first his knees passed under the stick, then his stomach, and then his chest. Then he stopped moving for a second as though he were about to fall backwards.

"Hang in there, Brother Plato," Brother Billy urged, as he clenched his fists nervously.

Winston inched forward as Mr. Soul looked on excitingly singing out the lyrics. Winston's neck was now under the stick less than an inch from touching it. *Come on, Winston,* he urged himself, *Keep your feet flat, you got less than a foot to go.*

"Go, Winston," Gloria cheered.

"You're nearly there!" Brother Pens yelled.

"Man, what's this dude doing?" Roll'em Rick asked Horno. "He's going to break his back."

The cheers and hollers were so loud, that you could barely hear the band as Winston inched closer, his eyes stared at the bamboo stick that was so close that his eyelashes touched it briefly. *Two more inches, don't blow it.* Winston scooted forward one more inch, and then one more inch, before jumping up with a sigh of relief.

Dancin' Beerwolf broke from the semicircle and rushed over to Winston. Nearly knocking him over, he gave Winston a big bear hug. "I knew you could do it, I knew you could do it."

"All right, everybody settle down," Mr. Soul ordered as Michael approached the bamboo stick. "You ready?" He asked.

"Let the music start," Michael answered as he reared his back as far as he could, quickly scooting forward at a much faster pace than Winston. "Let's get going, so we can get this stick lowered from its amateur level down to championship level." Michael hollered out confidently, but his eyes showed a little nervousness as he inched forward. In just seconds his stomach, and then his chest, and then his neck slid underneath the stick.

"You're almost there, Michael!" Laura yelled.

"It's a piece of cake, Michael!" One of the Delta's hollered.

The semicircle of fans moved closer as they cheered, and now they were only a few feet from the bamboo stick.

Michael inched forward, as perspiration poured from his face. The pressure on his thin legs was mounting as his eyes faced the bamboo stick directly above. Michael grimaced in pain, as his legs trembled with the strain.

"Go, Michael, go," Laura screamed to him as she moved closer. Michael less than two inches away, knowing that his legs were about to give out, gave one last scoot forward, but it was not enough, as his legs collapsed. He fell back slamming hard on the floor.

The Kappas cheered their victory, as they gathered around Winston. Michael slowly stood up. Rolling down his pant legs, he walked over and congratulated Winston. Then he pulled out $50 and handed it to Winston. "Good show, Winston," Michael conceded, but the good sportsman-like conduct ended with his parting jab, "Too bad it doesn't count toward intramurals this year, cause we're going to kick your ass for the second year in a row."

Winston just smiled as the Brothers booed Michael.

"Hey, sore loser," Brother Spoon yelled.

Winston taunted Michael as he turned to walk away, "What's it like, stallion breath, to take a sauna in a suit?"

Winston walked over to Mr. Soul, gave him a high five and a pat on the back, and then took the microphone.

"All right, Brothers," Winston announced waving the fifty dollar bill high in the air, "Drinks are on me."

The Kappas cheered as they headed for the mahogany bar. In the background Michael hurriedly put on his white coat as he marched out the door, with Laura and the others in close pursuit.

Gloria approached Winston and kissed him. "You're amazing, Brother Plato," she smiled shaking her head, "All that talent going to waste."

Winston just grinned, "One more beer and let's call it a night. I want to be nice and rested when I kick your cute ass on the slopes tomorrow."

Gloria laughed, "Dream on, Winston. You can't beat me, and you know it."

Chapter

Four

"Please, Gloria, this is the last time," Winston begged as they stood at the very top of the championship ski run, called Lonesome Quail, rated the most difficult run in all of New Mexico. "And besides you need to save your energy for later on tonight."

Gloria, as usual, acted like she didn't hear what Winston had just said. "Oh, Winston, look how beautiful it is out here," Gloria said as she brushed the snow off her navy down ski jacket, "and besides, you lucky devil, we are dead even. You have beaten me three times to my three. Isn't this so romantic?" Gloria stopped to gaze at the mountains, as she reached her hand out to catch the large soft falling snow. "And look down below at all the huge pine trees all covered with snow. It's like we are in a dream, it doesn't even look real."

"Gloria," Winston answered, putting his arm around her shoulder, "that's why I like you so much - so sensitive, so sweet, and so sentimental." He paused to grin at her and stared into her eyes, "How did you ever get hooked up with me?"

"Good question, Winston, good question," Gloria kissed Winston on the lips. "Maybe deep down I'm just a masochist."

Winston smiled, grabbed a handful of snow and threw it at Gloria, who ducked the shot just in time.

"Nice try, buddy," Gloria giggled, "but no cigar." She glanced around. "Can you believe it? We have practically had this run to ourselves. Where is everybody?"

"I don't know, must be something big going on in town is my only guess." Grabbed his ski pole that had been stuck in a drift. "That's all right with me. I don't need an audience to watch this slaughter that's fixin' to take place." He lowered his goggles, pushed hard on his ski poles and started down the steep slope.

"Damn you, Winston, you little cheat," Gloria hollered at him as she quickly followed in pursuit. "I'm still going to beat you." And off the pair skied, Gloria just a few yards behind. Down the championship back run with all its majestic beauty, they skied at record speed, doing jumps and dodging century old cedar trees as they descended. Seconds later they approached the most testing part of the ski run - nicknamed Hell's Corner, because of the abundance of cedars, and the narrowing pathway. Their speeds by now had approached a cautious maximum as they almost side by side made their way down, twisting, turning and zigzagging about. The soft fresh snow flew high in the air with such abundance that at times they could barely see ahead.

"I'm gaining on you, Mr. Jump the Gun," Gloria hollered to Winston as she approached not too far behind him. Winston raised his right pole in the air acknowledging her jab, but quickly turned to his left to avoid an old dying cedar tree that stood directly in front of his path. Then, his thoughts switched to his skiing companion as he turned his head back to see how Gloria was negotiating this tough stretch.

Just as he turned, a frightened young doe jumped up from a low growing cedar right in front of Gloria's direction.

"Look out, Gloria!" Winston hollered.

But it was too late, Gloria turned sharply to her left to avoid the collision, but in doing so she turned too fast, flipping up in the air and doing a back flip. She somehow landed on her skis but raced down the slope backwards with no poles. In shock, and slow to react to the situation, she kept skiing backwards.

"Turn, Gloria!" Winston hollered as he turned sharply to his left stopping just short of the Cedar. "Turn, damn it!"

Gloria snapped out of her daze turned around just in time for Winston to tackle her and prevent her head on collision into the cedar. They both tumbled through the snow like white boulders and came to a sliding stop directly in front of the huge cedar, whose two century old thick branches extended out from the trunk like a giant slingshot. Their skis and poles were scattered about like pickup sticks. Winston pulled Gloria up from the powdery snow, and removed her goggles. Wiping the snow from her face he asked, "Are you okay?"

Gloria remained limp, her eyes closed.

"For God's sake, Gloria," He shook her body vigorously, "Wake up, are you okay?"

Gloria slowly opened her eyes and smiled, "Hi, Winston."

"That's not funny, you scared me half to death."

"You deserved it, Mr. Jump the Gun," She laughed. "Oh, I guess I shouldn't be so hard on you. After all, you probably saved my life."

"It's going to cost you," Winston answered grinning. "It's going to take more than just saving my life."

"Just what is it going to take, my little chickadee?" Winston asked sarcastically.

She stood up and brushed the snow off her legs, and then reached over to the overhanging branch above Winston's head, shaking it furiously. The snow dumped onto Winston's face.

"Damn your little Peter Pan hide," Gloria spoke with true irritation. "When are you going to give it up?" Gloria stopped to pace back and forth, then stood in front of Winston, "You're in your fifth year and are barely a junior."

"Oh, Gloria, let's don't get serious now," Winston pleaded, "it's starting to snow again, and it's such a pretty day."

"Here we go again, changing the subject again aren't we?" Gloria paced about and then kicked snow on Winston's legs. "You never want to get serious, Winston, and that's what's wrong." Gloria shook her head in hopelessness. "It's no use. Why even try?" Winston did not say a word, just sat there with his patented sad puppy dog look.

Gloria, feeling sorry for Winston, sat down beside him and gently rubbed his right thigh, "Winston, sweetheart, you have too much going for you to wallow your life away hanging around these drunks and has beens," a tear trickled down Gloria's cheek as she spoke.

"Now, Gloria," Winston started but Gloria interrupted.

"I know, I'm nagging again. Give it up, for God's sake, please give it up," Gloria's eyes stared straight at into Winston's, without blinking once, "Not for me, honey, but for you."

"You're right," Winston admitted, "you're always right."

"You had a full golf scholarship to the University of Houston, and you let it slip away. Why?"

"We've discussed this issue before," Winston answered obviously not wanting to rehash it. "I was so good, I wanted to practice when I felt it was necessary," Winston slammed his fist against the cedar trunk, "but they didn't see it my way."

Gloria threw her arms up in the air. "Oh, God help us all, you didn't want to practice, so you blew a lifetime career because of that?"

Winston just blinked with a blank look on his face,

"Winston, you were better than Crenshaw and Kite," Gloria lectured, "you would be making a fortune by now."

"I don't want to hear anymore about it, Gloria," He ordered.

Gloria wrapped her arms around him, hugging his shoulders as tight as she could, "Oh, Winston, maybe I'm no fun anymore. Maybe you need to find yourself a party girl," Gloria shook her head again. "Last night was almost too much for me, watching a bunch of slobbering drunks make complete fools of themselves." Gloria stood. "Sorry, Winston, it's not funny to me anymore, it's embarrassing.

"You're right, Gloria," he agreed again.

"But what are you going to do about it?"

Winston walked a few feet away, picked up one of Gloria's skis, and calmly returned, "We have four more missing poles and three more skis to find." He put his left arm around her neck and gave her a big hug. "Gloria, I think I'm falling in love with you."

She just put her hand over her forehead in hopelessness. "Damn you, Winston, you eternal ostrich, you might as well stick that stubborn head of yours in a snow bank."

He just smiled.

"You're never going to change are you?" Gloria asked, but really didn't want to know the answer.

Winston remained silent.

"I give up," Gloria threw her arms up with disgust and walked back up the slope to look for her remaining poles and ski.

Winston chased her. "I'm coming to get you."

Gloria started running, finally stopping behind a small cedar tree. Hiding behind it, she yelled, "Leave me alone, just leave me alone."

Winston grabbed her right arm and pulled her gently down in the snow. They rolled over twice before they stopped with Winston lying directly on top of Gloria. He softly brushed her brown hair away from her eyes, then gently kissed her on her forehead, then her nose, and then several times on her lips.

"Gloria, I do like you very much, more than you think I do."

Gloria smiled, "Winston, you little devil. You remind me of a little boy with that silly grin of yours. Why do I like you so much?"

Winston pulled her up, and put his arms around her. "Let's get going. How about a nice candlelight dinner tonight - away from the zoo."

"Sure."

Chapter

Five

"All right, my fellow Brothers, the executive council is now in session." Winston Fox surveyed the six Brothers who were seated around the antique oak table that was located in the number one's room. Winston quietly lit a cigarette, and reviewed the Brothers before him. To his far left, Manse, was appointed for his common sense approach to situations, and for his ability to come up with logical solutions to problems. Next to him, was Brother Sabotage, basically the elected 'hit man' of the group. When things got rough or dirty, Troy was elected to execute the job. And to his left, good ol' Charlie The Spoon Luna. His appointment to the executive council, was quite obviously greed based. When situations got desperate, Charlie would be propositioned to fork out money. "Not this time, guys, my parents are going to find out." He would say over and over again. Next was Sgt. T. an executive member due to his ability to calmly study the problem that was being discussed, and present, in most cases, an intelligent solution. The other two remaining members were Billy The Kid and Dancin' Beerwolf. Their appointments needed no explanations.

Winston reached into the humidor that was on the table, and pulled out a thick Cuban cigar. Lighting it slowly, and savoring its taste, he said, "Well, Brothers, as we all know," he paused to blow several smoke rings up in the air, "We are going to have to come up with a plan to raise some serious dough. Anybody have any suggestions?"

Everyone remained silent, turning and looking at each other, hoping someone would speak out first. Finally Billy The Kid came up with an idea, "Brother Plato, the Ebony Golf Classic is being held this weekend at Apache Trails Municipal Golf Course."

"So?" Brother Beerwolf questioned.

Billy rose from his chair and paced around the table. "It means that my gamblin' black hustlin' friend, Bobby J., will be partners with his Lubbock buddy Scar. They have won it the last two years in a row. I say Winston and I take 'em on."

"Christ, Billy have you gone nuts?" Brother Beerwolf blurted out. "He runs all the whorehouses and nightclubs, and no tellin' what else in the Heights." Beerwolf shook his head as he continued, "Billy, he's too dangerous, and besides I've heard about Scar, didn't he just get out of prison?"

"Don't worry. Bobby J. is a friend and a fellow gambler just like me. There's a code of honor among us, he's not going to jack with us if we clip them, and besides I play with Bobby J. all the time, and so has Winston."

Winston interjected, "You might have an idea, Billy. So what is your plan?"

"I say after the Ebony Classic is over with, we set up a low ball high stakes golf game with them," Billy grinned with his usual confident look. "We can kick their asses, and if there are enough presses during the match, I figure we could win maybe $1,000, if we're lucky."

"Billy's right," Winston agreed. "I can beat Bobby J. on a regular basis. Scar I've never seen or played against," Winston paused, "but there's not a black Brother in this country that I can't beat."

Brother Beerwolf pounded his hands on the table, "That's the Kappa Kappa spirit, Brother Plato."

"How are you going to pay these dude's off if you lose $1,000?" Sgt. T. asked skeptically.

"Good question, Sgt. T.," Winston said. "It's very simple - we can't lose, and that's all there is to it." Winston stopped, a curious expression on his face. "Or we're up shit creek without a paddle."

"Let's go for it," Brother Sabotage offered.

Manse started to speak up, but instead just shook his head, knowing Winston had already decided and it was no use to try and dissuade him no matter how reckless this idea sounded.

"All in favor?" Winston quickly asked. Five hands shot up in the air, followed slowly by Manse's.

"All right, Winston, I will call Bobby J. in the morning and get the match set up. In the meantime, partner, I suggest that you start practicing your game," Billy stopped to smile, "which means you might have to skip a few classes."

"Kid, as you know, I just love to practice," Winston retorted. "Meeting adjourned."

Chapter

Six

It was a beautiful October day in the Texas Panhandle. October, because of its mostly mild temperatures, windless days, and Indian sunsets, was considered the best month of the year.

The temperature this Monday afternoon was above normal, almost reaching 80, and the wind was virtually nonexistent, only a gentle breeze would blow every so often.

"Couldn't pick a better day to kick their asses," Billy commented as he stood on the first tee box overlooking the front nine. "And can you believe it, the wind's not blowing 90 miles an hour."

"Quiet," Winston warned, "It will hear you."

Apache Trails was your typical West Texas golf course. It's

Bermuda fairways were lined with old untrimmed elm trees that were spaced apart like little soldiers as they pointed their way toward each slightly raised green ahead of them. Out of town golfers could be seen almost every day in the clubhouse shaking their heads as they went carefully over each and every hole on their scorecards. "Hell, this is too damn frustrating," one out of towner was overheard mumbling, "How the hell can you figure out which hole is which, when they all look the same?" Many of the local old time players pretty much hit the nail on the head when they came up with the nickname, Goat Patch Gardens for this not too picturesque municipal golf course.

"Quit your bitchin'," Ol' man Thomas would say over and over again, "At least the green fees are cheap."

It was not a very hard course, about normal yardage for most municipal courses, but there were more obstacles to conquer than most golfers were led to believe. Although the course had only 12 sand traps, they were death traps for those who had misfortune to land in one of them. The rocky sand was never raked and it's hardened appearance would literally wear you out mentally, as you tried to figure out the best way to escape one of these sand caked bunkers. Most golfers chose the smart answer - slam down hard on the putter, bouncing it over the grassy lips, and with a little luck, giving themselves at least a chance to make a long putt. Beside these West Texas sand traps, there were more hazards to deal with. Ground squirrels were everywhere and their burrowed holes dotted the course like acne on a 14 year old's face.

Time after time, a good round was lost, when an errant drive would disappear, just a yard or two from the fairway. And to top it off, there were the brown hawks, called kites, that nested on the large elm tree on the left of the eighth tee box. They would dive bomb players that wandered anywhere below their nest, and would attack the poor unsuspecting souls with such viciousness that they would many times bring on blood. "Oughta shoot the bastards," Gimpy, the greens keeper, would say over and over again, "but they are a protected species and the federal government won't let us do it."

Behind the seventh green was a fenced in prairie dog town that was interesting to first time players, but their noisy behavior was just irritating to most of the local players, but was a buffet for the two red foxes that made their home, or should we say den, on the washed out gully near No.11. They could be seen trotting about the course in search of their day's catch. Although you could not get to close to them, they never showed signs that the carts or the players that walked by bothered them.

On the first tee box, the players gathered to begin their low ball duel. Winston sat in his golf cart next to Gloria. In between them on the floorboard was an iced down cooler of beer. Winston preferred to ride a cart during his gambling matches, and unlike most other golfers, actually played better when he drank beer, as long as he paced himself carefully. Billy The Kid stood not far from the cart as his caddy Dancin' Beerwolf wiped off The Kid's persimmon driver. "We're gonna kick their ass!" Beerwolf whispered a little too loud.

"Sh,sh…" Billy replied as he stretched his legs and stared at the twosome in front of him, playing particular attention to Scar. "Damn, who the hell is this guy?" Billy mused as he studied his appearance. Scar looked like he belonged in a Mexican bullfight, but instead of playing the role of the bullfighter; he would better pass for playing the role of the bull.

"Looks like a walking icebox," Billy surmised as he stared at the deep scar on his face that started at the middle of his forehead, crossed his right eye and ended just below his right ear. Billy then turned to Winston, "What about this scar, Brother Plato, where the hell…"

Before he could finish, Winston interjected, "Don't ask, Kid, just play the golf course and everything else will fall into place."

Winston lit a cigarette, popped open a beer and patted Gloria on the left thigh, "Damn, Gloria, those yellow short shorts you are wearing are going to drive 'em crazy."

"And how about you?" Gloria answered with a curious grin.

Winston turned his attention to Bobby J. as he approached the golf cart. Bobby J. was nearing 60 in age, and his 5'8", 165 pound stature would fool you - he could still knock the hell out of the ball, and was one of the best putters and chippers that Winston had seen for a three handicapper.

"What's happenin', my friend?" Bobby J. just grinned as he shook Winston's hand, and gave Billy a high five. "You honkies ready to get your asses beat?"

Winston smiled as he answered, "What's the bet?"

"$200 a hole, low ball only, press when you're mad," Bobby J. offered his proposal, smiling confidently at his partner.

"You're on, Bobby J," Winston flipped his cigarette to the ground as he reached into his bag for his driver. "Much easier this way Kid, don't you think?"

Billy laughed quietly, knowing that he, like most scratch golfers preferred to walk. Rarely would you see a championship player ride a cart during a money match or a tournament, much less one with an iced down beer cooler below his feet.

Winston nonchalantly stepped out of the golf cart, yawned and then turned to Billy, "Let's get this pigeon shoot over with."

Bobby J. overhearing Winston's smart remark, just laughed. "Funny, funny aren't you, white boy?" Bobby J. walked over and patted Winston on the left shoulder. "You're going to be sippin' on pigeon soup from now on, after we clip your little white asses."

Winston and Billy both laughed at Bobby J.'s kidding remarks.

"Hit away, Bobby J," Winston motioned, "you all have the honors."

As Bobby J. walked toward his partner, Scar, Billy whispered in Winston's ear, "Damn, Brother Plato, have you noticed the stare on Scar's face. He hasn't smiled or said a word yet."

Winston popped open a beer, "Relax, Kid, this is just another one of Bobby J.'s tricks." He placed his beer on the top of the cart, and started gripping his driver, searching for the right feel. "Don't let 'em get the best of you." He slapped Billy on the back, "Wake up, Kid, remember your motto - never let them see you sweat."

Billy regaining his composure and let out a big grin, as he watched Scar burn the fairway with his big booming drive. Over twenty of the Kappa Kappa members showed up to follow Winston and Billy around to cheer them on in their quest for victory. On the other hand, Bobby J. and Scar, except for their caddies, had no following.

"Strange," Winston noted.

The first six holes passed quickly, with no blood exchanging hands. Nobody seemed loose, and few greens were hit in regulation.

Chatter and kidding went on as expected between Bobby J. and Winston and Billy. But throughout the match, Scar, remained silent other than cussin' loudly when he hit poor shots.

"He scares me, Winston," Gloria whispered as she grabbed Winston's right arm on the seventh tee box. "He looks like he belongs in solitary confinement somewhere."

"Well, it's for sure we won't see him hosting any game shows on TV anytime soon," Winston commented as he watched Bobby J. duck hook his ball into the elms on the left.

"Shit," Bobby J. mumbled.

Winston for the next three holes came alive. He birdied seven, sinking a 22 foot downhill curving putt.

"Way to go, Winston," Gloria hugged him as he sat back in the cart.

His iron shots were so precise into the No.8 green, and No.9 green, that they were within 'give me' range. Scar missed a short seven footer on No.9 to tie Winston's birdie, and threw his putter twenty yards back into the fairway, and stomped off the green, mumbling every curse word imaginable.

"Three birdies in a roll, Arnie Palmer," Billy high fived Winston's hand. "We got 'em three down, two down, and one down. We're up $600, so far."

Winston, with a serious look on his face, answered Billy, "Remember the great words of Socrates, oh Billy, my boy."

"What words?" Billy asked with interest.

"Don't count your chickens, before the eggs hatch."

Gloria laughed, and then offered encouraging words to Winston, "Come on, honey, you know you are the best. Show those University of Houston golf coaches why they should never have let you go." Gloria, generally much shyer as a rule, seemed to bubble with enthusiasm.

"No sweat, Sherlock, my dear," Winston smiled confidently at her and kissed her on the lips. "I have the most beautiful caddy in the world riding next to me. And damn those long dark perfectly shaped legs..."

"Stop it, Winston," Gloria ordered. "Time to focus your

concentration elsewhere."

Bobby J. approached the cart. "Nice playin, Arnie," Bobby J. congratulated Winston with a sarcastic grin on his face.

"But the fun is fixin' to happen."

"Any presses?" Winston asked.

"Not now," Bobby J. answered. "We'll let you know when we are ready."

Billy approached the cart and sat down next to Gloria as she scooted to her left. "He's up to something," Billy shook his head back and forth, "But I don't know what."

"Strange," Winston mused.

"What's the matter, honey?" Gloria asked.

"Strange that they wouldn't press on this hole."

Holes 10, 11, and 12 were completed, with neither of the duos gaining ground. Winston sank a long impossible 40 footer to tie Scar's par on No.12.

"Lucky mother fucker," was all Scar said as he marched off the green, while the Kappa cheering section whooped and hollered their support.

"Way to go, Brother Plato," Brother Spoon yelled as the foursome stood on the 13th tee box. The 13th hole was a straight away 311 yard par 4, that was drivable both for Scar and Winston today, but it was a gamble to attempt this effort, because less than 20 yards to the right of the green were three small mesquite bushes that lined up against a barb wire fence.

Beyond the fence were grazing cows that paid little attention to the out of bound golf balls that would come their way.

Billy hit first, sending his drive 255 yards straight down the middle. "All right, Winston, I played it safe. Now you can go for it."

"Put it on, Winston," Gloria urged as she clapped her hands.

Brother Roll 'em Rick standing in the small Kappa gallery in his black leather jacket, wearing his dark, thick large sunglasses joined in the fun. "Come on, dude," he encouraged Winston," put that white dude on the green."

Winston teed up his ball, backed away for a second to study his line, and then he ripped a huge drive down the right side of the fairway, the ball drawling in toward the middle.

"Great drive, Winston," Billy praised, "You're going to be right in the middle of the green."

Just as Billy finished, the hard bouncing ball hit something on the fairway and took a high bounce to the right, finally landing to the right of the green.

"Damn," Winston moaned, "Where the pin is today, it's Death Valley over there. No way I can get birdie from there, unless I sink a 50 footer coming back."

Winston returned to the cart and quickly lit up a cigarette.

"Sorry, honey," Gloria consoled him as she rubbed his back.

"Oh, well, that's the breaks," Winston smiled trying not to show disappointment.

"You were robbed," Billy commented as he walked over to Winston.

"Oh, well, you know what they say in the old country," Winston said turning to Billy.

"And what's that, Brother Plato?" Billy asked knowing another famous quote was coming his way.

"When in doubt, you just gotta blow that shit off."

Gloria laughed, "Oh, Winston get serious now."

Bobby J. hollered over to Winston, "What's the matter,

Winston, the golf Gods don't like you today?"

Winston ignored the jab, as he watched Bobby J. sky his ball high in the air, as it landed in the right rough barely 190 yards ahead.

"He who laughs best, laughs last," Winston muttered to Gloria, but made sure Bobby J. didn't hear him.

It was Scar's next shot as he studied his options with his skinny lookin' black caddy who was in his late teens, but as Winston had seen him play before, was a damn good golfer.

"I say, hit your driver, man," the skinny kid urged, "now is the time for a birdie. Put a little scare in these white boys' eyes."

Scar hesitated as he kept switching clubs in his bag, "I say I hit my one iron, as hard as that fairway is, I will be right in front of the green."

"Hit your driver, man, and be done with it," His caddy urged.

"Hit your driver, Scar," Bobby J. agreed, "Let's show these honkys whose boss around here."

Scar took a huge cut at the ball that drilled through the air like a rifle shot. They both watched the ball stop just short of the green and then bounce hard as it rolled quickly through the green.

"Stop, you mother…" Scar stopped in mid sentence as he watched his drive shoot through the green down the right slope, as it kept bouncing for the mesquite bushes ahead. Then he lost sight of it.

"Is that mother in bounds?" He asked growling the words out to his caddy.

"It's still in," His caddy nervously answered, scared to death that his answer would be wrong.

"It better be," Scar warned as he slammed his driver against the bag.

Bobby J. approached his short drive as the others waited behind him. He then pulled out a nine iron and practiced several swings before lining up his shot. "Gotta hit a knock down shot with this deadpan lie," he told Scar just before he hit down through the ball. His hips moved too fast, causing him to shank the ball low and to the right. He angrily watched his ball roll on and on, until it finally stopped just a foot from Winston's ball.

Bobby J. showed no signs of frustration as he slowly walked toward Billy's ball, instead whistled calmly.

"All right, Billy," Winston whispered with encouragement, "we got 'em, unless Scar somehow has a shot out of the mesquite jungle up there. Just an easy sand wedge right in the middle of the green," Winston advised. "Don't get cute."

"I wasn't born yesterday," Billy replied smiling, as he lined up to hit his shot.

"Perfecto, Kid," Winston praised as he watched Billy's high wedge shot hit softly on the green some 20 feet below the pin.

All four of the players walked forward to find Scars misplaced drive. Seconds later, Scar stood by the barb wire fence staring at his ball that was just two feet beyond. He then turned to Slim his caddy and grabbed him. "You stupid son of a bitch! I told you I shouldn't hit a driver on this hole." Scar, in a mad rage, threw his caddy down hard on the ground.

"Sorry," was all Slim could say as he laid in the dirt.

"Shit!" Scar yelled as he unzipped the side of his golf bag.

"What the hell is he doing?" Billy whispered to Winston. "A new ball is not going to do him any good here. He's got to go back to the tee box and re-hit."

"Sh," Winston calmly replied as he watched Scars tantrum with concern.

"Winston, that's not a ball he's pulling out of his bag, that's a damn .357 Magnum," Billy whispered.

Scar took three steps forward, aimed the gun right at his ball, and fired at it, blowing it high in the air. He fired three more times at the pieces, until there was hardly anything left of the ball to shoot at. The grazing cattle not far away, took off in all directions.

"Cool it, Scar," Bobby J. ordered, "you're gonna start a stampede."

"I don't give a damn," Scar answered as he stared down his opponents. He then flashed two fingers at them letting them know that there were still two bullets left.

Billy jumped on the back of the cart with Beerwolf to his side ready to ride quickly away from Scar. "Damn, Winston, this guy is crazy," Billy warned as he wiped the perspiration from his forehead.

"Winston, forget the match," Gloria begged, "let's get out of here."

Winston showed no sign of emotion, instead just smiled.

"Calm down, Kid, this is nothing more than a dog and pony show that Bobby J. has dreamed up. He's just trying to psych us out."

"Well, he's doing a damn good job of it," Billy answered, motioning to Winston to give him a drag from his cigarette.

"Billy, I never knew you smoked," Winston said.

"I just took up the habit," Billy replied.

"Good par, Billy," Winston praised as they approached the 14th tee box. "You had me worried for a minute there, leaving that 20 footer eight feet short."

"Don't even remember it going in," Billy answered as he fiddled with golf club.

The Kappa gallery behind them didn't move forward, instead they stayed well back of the 14th tee box. Not a sound or a cheer was heard from the small gathering until finally Roll'em Rick spoke, "I've had enough of this shit, man." Rick adjusted his sunglasses as he started walking away. "This dude is outta here."

Bobby J. with an almost devilish look on his face approached the cart.

"Sorry about my man, Winston," Bobby J. apologized. "Good sportsmanship is just not his bag."

"Forget it," Winston calmly answered as he popped open a beer.

"Let's see," Bobby J. continued as he studied the scorecard. "You got us four down, three down, two down, and one down. Is that not correct?"

"Right on target, Bobby J.," Winston verified.

"Then we're gonna throw four presses at you boys' lily white asses," Bobby J. laughed with a sinister grin.

"You're on, Bobby J." Winston answered with authority. "But something is troubling me."

"And what's that?" Bobby J. asked with a puzzled look.

"I don't know where I'm going to find an armored car to haul off all our winnings."

"Funny, funny, aren't you white boy," Bobby J. laughed as he spoke, "But as you have said before yourself, it ain't over 'till the fat lady sings, right Winston?"

Winston didn't answer just slowly got out of the cart and approached the blue tee markers.

"Let her rip, Winston," Beerwolf hollered, as he watched Winston's drive land 270 yards down the right side of the fairway.

Thirty minutes later, Billy and Winston walked off the 17th green with their heads down in shock.

"Damn it, Winston, we're choking all to hell," Billy pitched his putter angrily at his bag. "I can't believe it. We've lost four holes in a row."

Winston didn't answer, for the first time that Gloria could remember, he was totally lost for words.

Billy continued, "Everything that could possibly go wrong has gone wrong. First, Scar sinking that 50 foot putt on 14 to beat us. Then, Bobby J. holing out that impossible bunker shot on 15." Billy shook his head hopelessly, "He hit that pin so hard it nearly knocked it over, but it still went in."

Winston remained silent as he approached the golf cart.

"And then I gave 'em 16 and 17, missin' those short putts." Winston sat in the cart, and without looking at Gloria, lit up a cigarette and took a sip from his beer.

"You okay, Winston?" Gloria asked as she put her arm around him.

"I guess," Winston rolled his cigarette back and forth between his fingers. "Bobby J.'s psyche job is working quite well, and Billy is no help. He hasn't been the same since Scar pulled that gun trick back on 13." Winston stared over at the 18th tee box. "And now all their Brothers from the Heights have suddenly shown up. Must be at least 50 of them. Another clever ploy by Bobby J."

Winston shook his head, but then managed a grin. "Oh, hell, it's just money."

"But, how are you going to pay off if you lose?" Gloria asked almost in tears.

"Oh, hell, Gloria, I won't worry about that today, I will worry about that tomorrow." Winston gained his composure as Bobby J. sauntered up to the cart.

"Well, Winston, since we put four presses on you boys back on 14, I show we got you closed out on six bets, one up on another one, and even on the other bet. Is that the way you see it?" Bobby J.'s eyes gleamed with delight as Scar stood quietly in the background with his ominous penetrating stare.

"That's correct, Bobby J.," Winston answered calmly. "You know, you would have been a pretty good accountant in your younger days."

Bobby J. smiled and asked."So?"

"So, my man, we press all out bets." Winston didn't blink an eye as he said this.

"So as I see it," Bobby J. continued as he leaned his hand on the top of the golf cart, "You lose the hole, you lose $2,800. You tie us, you lose $1,400. Is that not correct?"

"You left out one slight detail, my man," Winston shot back trying to show coolness in his voice.

"And what's that?" Bobby J. replied.

"If we win the hole, which we will, you're going to owe us $200."

"This is a lot of money we're talking about, Winston," Bobby J. warned as he slapped his hand on Winston's shoulder, "you know, Scar don't take too kindly to people that don't pay off their gambling losses. You sure about all these presses?"

Winston smiled with a cocky flair, "You all have the tee box. Let's get this show on the road, you're starting to cut into my partying time."

Bobby J. just laughed as he approached the tee box and whispered into his partner's ear.

"Winston, what are you going to do?" Gloria asked with a frantic look on her face.

"It's not good, that's for sure, honey," Winston answered. We have our backs against the wall. This hole is a par 5 with a small pond in front," Winston paused as he popped open another beer.

"Go on," Gloria urged.

"It's pretty much a birdie hole for all of us, which means the only way Billy and I can keep from losing our asses is to somehow eagle it."

"I don't understand," Gloria asked in total confusion.

"Don't worry, my fair maiden," Winston offered his condolences. "It's very simple, I am just going to have to eagle the little bugger."

"Oh, Winston, damn you, why did I even come?" Gloria put her hands over her face, "Why, oh why, do I subject myself to this stupid torture?"

Billy, walked over to Winston, "Did I hear you say that we are pressing all out bets?" Billy asked with his hands moving about nervously.

"That's a rog, Kid," Winston answered, confirming the bet.

"Christ, Brother Plato, we're diggin ourselves a deeper hole."

"Or grave," Gloria chimed in. "And I don't mean that to be funny."

Winston jumped out of the cart and high fived Billy, "Keep the faith, Brother," Winston encouraged as he stared down the narrow fairway ahead. "I've eagled this hole before, and I will just have to eagle it today." Winston turned to Billy as his face wrinkled with a serious look, "You're job, Billy, is to get your act together, and quit dwelling on the negatives."

"You're right, Winston. I'm okay now," Billy assured him, "Scar is not going to get on my nerves anymore."

"And what about that black gallery over there who will probably be trying to break our concentration?"

"From this moment forward, Arnie, I am Jack Nicklaus," Billy said, as he tried to imitate his idol's hawkish look.

"Get 'em, Jack," Winston urged. "You're job, Golden Bear, is to make damn sure you get a birdie here, that will at least tie their low ball, unless some miracle happens for us, and they make par or worse."

Bobby J. took a practice swing, and then addressed his ball.

"You're the man," a huge, burly black man yelled out from the gallery.

"Kick their asses," another man screamed out as loud as his voice would allow, as the rest of the black gathering around him, hooped and hollered their approval.

Winston, Billy, and Gloria, sitting close together in the cart watched Bobby J.'s drive sail down the middle of the 530 yard par 5, landing some 265 yards from the water protected green. The gallery roared their approval, as they high fived each other, and repeatedly yelled, "You're the man."

Scar then ripped another one of his low screaming cuts, his ball also finding the fairway, but some 40 yards farther.

Scar, for the first time today, smiled as he slapped Bobby J. on the back, and then turned and stared at Winston and Billy.

"All right, Jack," Winston motioned, "This is the 18th hole of the Masters, nobody can handle the pressure to win this tournament but you or me."

Billy, with a sudden boost of confidence, walked to the tee

box and addressed his ball with a near perfect swing.

"Great drive, Jack," Winston hollered as he jumped out of cart to congratulate the smiling Billy. "285 yards, straight down the middle."

Winston, without stalling a second, quickly teed his ball up, and with not one practice swing, swung as hard as he could. The momentum from his swing was so intense that his right foot spun out of control as he watched his drive slowly draw the right side precariously close to the overhanging tree branches.

"Hook, you son of a bitch," Winston begged as he leaned his to the left. "Hook, damn it, hook!" Winston again begged knowing full well that the only chance that he had to eagle was to hit a drive far enough that he could go for the green in two. "Hook, damn it, hook," He pleaded again as he watched his ball ignore his demands ricocheting through the stretched elm branches ahead.

"Damn it," Winston cursed as he watched his ball nosedive into the trees and slowly bounce almost to a standstill, until suddenly it took a large bounce in the air, and continued to bounce forward, making a loud noise like a ping pong ball.

"You lucky son of a bitch," Bobby J. moaned. "His fuckin' ball is bouncing down the cart path."

Winston couldn't believe his good fortune as he watched his pushed drive finally stop slightly inside the right cart path 320 yards away.

"Just as I had planned," Winston commented, as he smirked at Bobby J. who stood nearby just shaking his head in amazement. Winston calmly walked off the tee box and sat next to Gloria.

"Way to go, Arnie!" Billy hollered.

Winston lit a cigarette, took a sip of beer, and then

answered, "I was a little lucky there, Jack, but at least it gives me a chance to go for the green in two.

Winston drove down the cart path, until he approached the three balls that were lying in the middle of the fairway - all within 15 yards of each other. He then pulled the cart under one of the large elm trees.

"Nice and shady, here," Winston commented as he patted Gloria on the left shoulder.

"How are we doing, Winston?" Gloria asked not fully understanding what was going on.

"A mere formality here, my sweet," Winston informed her as he took a deep drag from his cigarette, and blew it out to his left.

"Winston, when are you going to quit those nasty things?" Gloria asked, fanning her hands at the smoke.

"As soon as I get rich," he answered with a grin. He turned around and watched all three players hit perfect layup shots, just short of the reed covered pond that guarded the front of the 18th green.

"Birdie city," Winston mumbled out loud.

"What on earth are you talking about, honey?" Gloria asked.

"They're all in perfect position. The pin's on the back side, and all they got to do is hit run up shots over the pond. They'll have putts of ten feet or less."

Billy walked over to the cart and hopped in next to Gloria as Brother Beerwolf stood quietly near them. Winston drove the cart slowly up the cart path, stopping just behind his ball.

He then approached his ball, studied his shot, walked back to the cart, and reached for his beer.

"Well, Jack, we're in luck," Winston smiled. "I've got a

great lie, the ball is sitting up nicely, slightly uphill." Winston paused to reach into his bag to pullout his three wood. "Shouldn't be any problem at all," he stated confidently, "Just a nice smooth 210 yard three wood shot rising high in the air over the pond ahead and landing softly some ten feet or less from the pin."

"You can do it, Arnie," Billy encouraged Winston, as he gave him a thumbs up motion.

Bobby J. sauntered over toward the cart. "Need to borrow a bazooka?" He asked Winston with a teasing smile.

Winston, showing no emotion, just took a sip of his beer and placed it on top of the cart. "Bobby J. my man," Winston grinned, "Have you ever seen a hot air balloon land softly on the ground during an Albuquerque balloon festival on a windless, sunny October day?"

Bobby J. just stared at Winston with a confused look.

"Well, I'm fixin' to show you what it would be like to see one, as I land this little white balloon softly on its target."

The Kappa gallery had gathered around, and clapped their hands with approval.

"You can do it, Brother Plato," Manse hollered.

Gloria jumped out of the cart, walked around to Winston, and whispered to him, "Go get 'em, Arnie," she encouraged with a big smile, and then walked back to the cart, sitting down on Winston's side.

Bobby J. just laughed as he started walking away. "A white balloon, eh?" Bobby J. started shaking his head, "What next, my man? You gonna start seeing bats and snakes? You better quit slurpin' on that booze. I'm startin' to worry about you."

"You play your game, Bobby J. and I will play mine," Winston answered chuckling, and then addressed his ball.

"Prepare for takeoff," Brother Spoon hollered, as the gallery behind him shushed him.

"Quiet everyone," Manse ordered as they eagerly watched Winston's do or die three wood shot.

"Please, Winston," Gloria pleaded in a soft whisper. "Please do it."

Billy stood leaning against the cart, nervously chewing on his left thumbnail. "Come on, Arnie, it's the Masters," He spoke loud enough for Winston to hear.

Without hesitating, for fear that he would eventually talk himself out of a good shot, Winston quickly ripped through the ball. Again it started high right hooking slowly left into the mild right to left wind.

"Blow, wind, blow," Winston begged as he watched his shot fly toward the green, "Hook you son of a bitch. Go!" Winston felt that he didn't get all of the shot, even though he made contact.

"Ain't got enough zip, Winston," Bobby J. hollered. "Ain't gonna take it."

As the ball made its final descent toward the front of the green, a small gust of wind came up.

"Blow, wind, blow," Winston again urged as he watched the ball momentarily disappear into the thick high reeds at the back of the pond.

"Damn it," Winston moaned as his ball remained out of sight.

"You know how to swim, Win…" before Bobby J. could finish his sentence, he watched Winston's ball suddenly appear on the green. "That mother is rollin at the fuckin' pin."

"Hey, Arnie," Billy screamed as he ran up beside Winston. "That son of a bitch almost hit the pin."

The Kappa gallery hooped and hollered, as Gloria leaped from the cart and ran over and hugged Winston.

"We ain't there yet," Winston warned, "There's still a little work to do."

Bobby J. and Scar remained shocked and quiet as they walked toward their second shots. Billy and Beerwolf walked several yards behind, being careful not to get too close.

"We got 'em by the balls, Kid," Brother Beerwolf whispered to Billy.

"Not yet, Beerwolf," Billy warned as he got a closer look at Winston's ball. "Looks like he's got a downhill slider, some seven or eight feet away." Billy paused as he stopped to watch Bobby hit his short approach shot over the pond that was just a few yards ahead of all three of their balls.

Bobby J. trying to hit a knock down shot, again spun out his hips too quickly, and watched in horror as the ball lined drive low and sliced right, slamming hard into the tall reeds in the middle of the pond, and then dropping straight down.

"You dumb mother fucker," Scar slammed his nine iron down on the ground, as he cursed with anger. "You shanked the mother again."

A small cry of surprise came from the Kappa gallery.

"Quiet," Winston ordered.

The black gallery that had gathered to the left of the fairway, moaned and groaned their disappointment.

"Come on, Scar, get it close," one cute black girl hollered out as she watched Scar prepare to hit.

"You're the man," was shouted out several times from the gallery.

Winston turned to Gloria, "We could get really lucky here, if Scar doesn't knock this close. I could two putt and win the hole." Winston reached over and grabbed Gloria's left hand, squeezing it firmly, and then whispered in a low voice, "Come on, Scar, chilly dip that little puppy right in the pond."

Scar lined up his shot, and then swung through the ball. He watched with anticipation as his knock down shot flew over the pond, and rolled toward the pin.

"Roll you little mother," He said as his ball rolled past the pin, stopping a foot by it, almost in front of Winston's line.

"You're my man," Bobby J. proudly yelled as he walked over and Scar a high five. Hoots and hollers screamed from the black gallery.

"I told you Scar, honey, that you was the man," the cute black girl hollered.

Billy, next up, wasted no time in hitting his shot, watching it also follow virtually the same path that Scar's ball took, landing a foot or so to the left of the pin.

Billy walked over toward Winston, "Damn, Winston, if that was on line that could have gone in."

Billy walked forward around the pond, with Brother Beerwolf walking to his side. "Great shot, Billy," Beerwolf praised.

"It doesn't mean a damn thing, unfortunately," Billy answered.

"The whole damn farm is on Brother Plato's shoulders. He can't miss that putt, or our ass is grass."

Winston drove down the right cart path, stopping just a few yards from the green. The Kappa gallery hurriedly followed.

"Gotta make this slithery little seven footer, Gloria, my love."

Gloria's smiles turned to frowns, as she suddenly realized what would happen to them, if he missed.

"My God, Winston," she asked, her hands trembling in fear. "Where are you going to come up with $1,400 if you miss?"

"No bad vibes, honey," Winston snapped back. "No bad vibes. We will give them the $400 in cash that we got on us, and I will I just have to write Bobby J. a hot check." Winston paused to take a sip from his beer. "The bank is closed. They won't know until in the morning that the check is hot."

"Winston, damn you," Gloria lectured as she hit his right shoulder. "Doesn't Scar kill people that do that to him?"

"Not if he can't catch 'em," Winston answered as he lit up a cigarette.

"What do you mean by that?" Gloria asked suspiciously.

"It means that we're gonna high tail our asses out of town awhile and pay Brother Surf an extended visit until we can figure some way to come up with the dough, if I miss."

"And what about your classes?" Gloria asked.

"Well, we will just have to put them on the back burner for a while," Winston paused as he reached for his beer, knowing what was coming next.

Gloria shook her head in disbelief, "I don't believe what I'm hearing, even though I should have known by now. You're risking your future, your life, over one stupid damn putt. Is that what you're telling me, Winston?"

Winston turned his head away and stared across the green at his ball. "Well, it just turned out this way, Gloria, but I guess you pretty much hit the nail on the head." Winston slowly got out of the cart and turned to Gloria, "Keep the faith, baby," he urged, "Keep the faith."

"Then what?" She demanded.

Winston grabbed his putter and his beer, and walked away

with his cigarette hanging out of the left side of his mouth. He turned back to face Gloria, "And then, we will just have to blow that shit off."

Gloria did not answer, nor did she even look at Winston, instead she crawled out of the cart and walked briskly away toward the large elm ahead, sat down beside it and leaned her back against the trunk.

Winston slowly sauntered on the green, joining up with the other players. Billy had already picked his ball up, after Bobby J. had given it to him, but Scar's putt was not as close as he bent down to measure the distance with his putter.

Winston, observing that Scars ball was 'in the leather,' motioned to him, "Pick it up, that's good."

Scar did not answer as he picked up his ball and threw it at the black gallery that had gathered around the left side of the green. Then he reached into his left pocket and pulled out a switchblade knife.

"Oh, shit," Beerwolf moaned, "Here we go again."

"Allow me to fix my divot," Scar said as he popped the six inch blade out, and repaired his ball mark. Then he turned to Winston, "Not used to repairing holes I make, this is kinda new to me." Scar commented with a sarcastic smile, as he turned and walked away.

Bobby J. watched Winston line up his curling downhill seven foot putt. Winston studied the putt, put his beer down, and laid completely flat on the ground behind his ball as he carefully tried to figure out the break.

Bobby J. walked over beside Winston, "Be careful, Winston, I don't want you to spill your pacifier."

"Always a clown, aren't you?" Winston asked, as he slowly stood up. Taking one last drag from his cigarette, he blew smoke rings high up in the still air, at the same time he reached down, grabbed his beer and chugged the last few ounces. He crushed the can and pitched it behind him off the green.

"You know, Bobby J., I sure could use some more beer money."

Bobby J. just grinned, "My partner is getting a little nervous. He wants to know how you honkys are going to fork out $1,400."

"Well, Bobby J," Winston answered coolly, "you know, it's not that big a deal, is it?" He asked. "Hell, it's just money."

Winston walked around the hole and lined up his putt from the back side, as all the other players walked off the green. The usual chatter from the two galleries was nonexistent. It was almost eerie to Winston, everything about him remained quiet and motionless, even the damn West Texas wind.

"Strange," Winston noted to himself as he studied the putt, "I feel like I'm in a damn mortuary." Winston walked back around to his ball, and addressed it as he prepared to putt.

Taking a few practice putts back and forth, just as he was about to putt, he stopped and backed off to rethink his putt's direction. In doing so, his mind lost concentration, and wandered about as if he were a lab dog chasing butterflies in a field. All his past failures flashed before his eyes. First, the called third strike that cost their All Star little league team the championship.

Suddenly freezing up in his sophomore speech class as he was suppose to speak on factory pollution - stage fright to the tenth degree. Winston shook his head in embarrassment as he recalled this humiliating failure. More flashbacks continued like a newsreel before his eyes - all with embarrassing results.

Stop it, he ordered his thoughts. *Stop it, you dumb shit.*

"Arnie," Billy spoke out with concern. "The Master's award ceremony is waiting for you. Sink the Goddamn putt, and be done with it."

Winston snapped back to reality, as he realigned his putt. *Come on, Arnie,* he coached himself, *sink the putt like you a ways do.* Then he smiled. *Make Jack jealous, and let him know that Arnold Palmer is still the King.*

Without hesitating, and without another practice stroke, Winston, or should we say Arnie, hitched his pants up, lined up his putt, and stroked it gently, as he watched the tricky fast moving downhiller curve toward the cup.

"Go in," Winston urged as he motioned with his putter.

The ball slowly rolled toward the cup, and finally curved in toward the hole.

"Go in," Billy begged as he watched Winston's putt horseshoe around the cup, and finally drop in. "You did it, Arnie." He screamed, as he rushed over and gave Winston a big hug. "You did it."

The Kappa gallery rushed across the green, yelling and hollering at their hero - almost knocking him down as they embraced him.

Winston smiled, and then turned his attention to Gloria, who remained emotionless as she sat by the tree with her arms crossed.

Brother Beerwolf jumped up on Winston like a little kid, "You did it, Brother Plato. You did it."

Winston pushed him off, "Down, Yogi Berra, down."

Bobby J. slowly walked over to Winston and whipped out a thick wad of money. Peeling off two one hundred dollars bills, he handed them to Winston.

"You're a lucky little white boy," Bobby J. grinned shaking his head. "You never could have had a chance to reach the green in two, if your ball hadn't a bounced down the cart path."

Bobby J. kept shaking his head, "And your ball never would have cleared that pond on your second shot, if it were not for that sudden burst of wind."

Winston just grinned as he answered, "I guess, my man, the golf Gods had a change of heart."

"Out of curiosity," Bobby J. asked, "how were you going to come up with the $1,400, if you missed that putt?"

"You know that I would have come up with the money," Winston answered, "one way or another."

"I know you would," Bobby J. agreed as he shook Winston's hand.

"Hell of a show, white boy," Bobby J. congratulated Winston, "But you're still a lucky little boy."

"I'd rather be lucky than good," Winston answered as he walked toward Manse.

"Here's $150 dollars. A small down payment toward the General's Ball, at least it's a start. The other $50 goes to my caddy, Gloria."

Winston walked off the green, and quietly approached Gloria. "Here's $50 for you, my fair maiden caddy," Winston handed the $50 dollar bill to Gloria, who still remained, hands folded, and leaning against the tree.

"Great performance, Winston," Gloria congratulated. "Instead of hiding out in Taos for the rest of the semester hoping that Scar won't track you down and kill you, you're up $200 dollars." Gloria stood up and slapped her hand against the tree, "Winston, damn you," Gloria admonished as she stuck the $50 in her right pocket, and put her arms around him. "Why, oh why…"

"No bad vibes, my lady, no bad vibes."

Chapter

Seven

"All right, my fellow Brothers, the executive council is now in session," Winston Fox announced with authority. Winston paused to relight his cigar. "As we all know, Brother Kid and I didn't exactly rob Fort Knox on our first plan to raise money for the General's ball." Winston paused as he puffed on his cigar, "So any new suggestions or ideas?"

The six executive council Brothers sat silently before him. Finally, Brother Sabotage spoke, "I've been mowing ol' man Howell's yard for the last two years, everybody knows how rich that son of a bitch is."

"So what are you getting at?" Manse asked.

"Well, he owns two Siberian huskies that he adores so much that you would think that they were his children."

Brother Sabotage paused thinking through his plan. "I say we catch them and hold them for reward money."

"That's kidnapping," Manse answered with a shocked look on his face.

"Ah, Brother Pens," Sabotage replied. "We're just gonna borrow the dogs for a couple of days."

Winston's curiosity was aroused. "And?" he asked.

Sabotage continued, "We keep them until we return them for reward money." Sabotage stopped to display his sadistic smile. "I figure he will at least offer $1,000 a piece for them if we play our cards right."

"And how are we going to go about this?" Winston asked.

Sabotage smiled as he answered, "Every night right before sunset, the ol' man takes his dogs for a walk over to Lipscomb Lake, which is not far from his five acre estate. He lets them run wild ahead of him, and then rounds them up a few minutes later. During this time, I say, we load 'em up in our car and haul ass."

"How the hell are you going to do that?" Brother Spoon asked.

"No sweat, Sherlock," Sabotage shot back. "They know me, and they love turkey legs. They'll follow me, anytime, like a Pied Piper, as long as I have a turkey leg as a carrot stick to lead them."

"Hell, man, we're Kappa Kappas," Charlie The Spoon Luna blurted out, "we can't resort to kidnapping."

"Cool your jets," Brother Sabotage shot back. "Ol' man Howell has screwed everybody that he has ever had dealings with. He's declared bankruptcy at least three times that I know of in all of his clever spin-off corporations. He's the biggest crook that ever walked the earth."

Winston pounded his gavel on the mahogany table, "I say we go for it."

Manse, as usual, started to question the idea, "I think we…"

Winston interjected, "All in favor?"

Five hands, as usual, shot up in the air, but this time Manse's hand didn't follow.

"All right, then it's a done deal," Winston pounded his gavel again on the mahogany table. "Brother Sabotage, I appoint you leader of this covert operation and Brother Sgt. T. you're second in command. Meeting adjourned."

Chapter Eight

Highland Park Gardens is a very exclusive, small residential area located in the historic district of Amarillo. It's towering street lined elm trees form a canopy high above over the brick laid streets that were built in 1929.

On the west side of the neighborhood is a beautiful lake surrounded by magnificent gardens, sculptures, and fountains. As the bright sun made its final descent in the distant sky, a 1961 Chrysler slowly drove down Churchill street. No one paid particular notice to the old beat up car with its rusted out back fenders, and it's broken back window.

"Another maid heading home," William Ford III noticed, as he watched the car turn left and disappear. "Wish the help would take a Goddamn bus, and keep their trashy cars out of sight," he mumbled to himself as he motioned for his poodle to come indoors. The car moved on, as it headed for the lake. On its back bumper were two faded bumper stickers. On the left side was a sticker that said, "Honk, if you love peace and quiet." On the right side of the bumper was a sticker that said, "Honk, if you're an alcoholic." Fortunately, the daylight was almost gone, and no one could read their messages.

"Looks like poodle city," Brother Sabotage commented as he popped open a beer.

"You're driving, remember?" Sgt. T. reminded him as he sat seriously in the shotgun seat, observing ol' man Howell in the far distance, walking his two prize Siberian huskies.

"Well, if it isn't Hansel and Gretel," Sgt. T. observed as he watched the two dogs run ahead, like two Alaskan sled dogs that had just broken loose.

"Check those dudes out, man." The lone occupant of the car's back seat motioned with his hand, "They're runnin' faster than jackrabbits."

"How the fuck would you know, Rick?" Sgt. T. asked sarcastically. "How can you see anything through those sunglasses?"

"Let's get serious," Brother Sabotage ordered as he parked the car, not far from the lake ahead. Quickly the two jumped out of the car, and ran toward the edge of the lake.

"Got the turkey leg?" Sabotage asked Sgt. T.

"Yeah," Sgt. T. said, "I've got the leashes and the leg."

Brother Roll'em Rick remained in the backseat, as he nervously watched the street behind him. The two crouched down low, as they waited for the dogs arrival.

"Here they come," Sgt. T. warned as he watched the two huskies dash toward the lake and splash into the water.

"Damn it," Sgt. T. moaned. "Where did those fuckin'

mallards come from?" He shook his head in frustration, as he watched the two dogs swim about chasing after the ducks. "Those dogs never go in the water."

Sgt. T. turned around to see where ol' man Howell was.

"We gotta move fast," he ordered as he hollered out to the two dogs waving the turkey leg high in the air.

"Come on, Hansel, come on Gretel, turkey anyone?"

The two dogs recognizing Sgt. T., and smelling the turkey leg, dashed out of the water, and ran toward him.

"Down boys," Sgt. T. whispered, as Brother Sabotage somehow managed to put leashes on both the dogs.

"Let's haul ass," Sgt. T. ordered as the two dragged the soaking wet dogs toward the car.

Looking back, Sgt. T. whispered as they loaded the two dogs in the backseat, "Just in time. Here comes the old man now."

Sabotage pressed the gas pedal down hard, as the car sped away.

"Easy, don't overdo it," Sgt T. warned, "We don't want to draw attention."

Sabotage eased up his speed as the Chrysler turned right and slowly drove away.

"Just in time," Sgt T. commented as the car slowly drove out of the exclusive neighborhood, "Just in time."

"Get these fuckin' dudes, off my ass," Roll'em Rick moaned as he backed up against the left door. The two huskies jumped up and down in the back seat, fighting over the turkey leg, their wet hair splashing water all over the car.

Sgt.T. reached back to restrain them, but his efforts were of little use, as he watched Hansel slap against Rick, knocking his sunglasses off, as he tried helplessly to get out of their way.

Chapter Nine

Winston sat quietly on his bed, as he reached down and pulled a beer out of the ice chest, lighting up a cigarette at the same time, he picked up the phone and called Gloria.

"Hello?" Gloria softly answered.

"My, what a sexy voice," Winston commented as he took a deep drag from his cigarette.

"Hi, Winston. What's Up?"

"There's the Kappa beer bust tomorrow night at the Thompson ranch..." before Winston could finish Gloria interrupted.

"So?" she asked in a what's-the-big deal voice. "What do you want me to do," she asked sarcasticly, "Show up and jump naked out of a cake?"

"Funny, funny, my dear," Winston laughed, "Come to think of it you would look pretty good all iced up with frosting."

"Only in your dreams, Brother Plato," Gloria answered.

"Gloria, I'm not going. Instead, I want you to come over and we will have a quiet evening alone - just the two of us." Winston paused to sip on his beer, "I will have the best champagne and snacks waiting for you - and a beautiful fire and music by Santana softly playing. What do you say?"

"Am I hearing you right, Winston?" Gloria asked with skepticism. "You're going to skip your fall beer bust at the ranch, to spend an evening with me?"

"That's correct," Winston confirmed.

"What are all your Brothers going to say about this?"

"They'll just have to get over it," Winston paused to take a deep drag from his cigarette, and continued. "And oh, by the way, you know something?" Winston asked with a slight hesitation in his voice.

"What, Winston?" Gloria asked.

"I love you."

Gloria couldn't believe what she was hearing. "You really do?"

"Of course, I do."

"I love you to, you little devil." Gloria replied as tears streamed down her cheeks. "Oh, Winston, I've been thinking," she hesitated.

"What Gloria?"

"Well, I don't know why I didn't, well you know, on the ski trip last weekend," Gloria hesitated again and then continued, "Well, Mary Lamb is the only other girl in my sorority that hasn't... well, you know what I'm getting at."

Winston jumped up, knocking his beer over in the process.

Hardly believing what Gloria had just told him, he replied in a low soft voice. "Oh, Gloria, we will have a great evening together, I promise."

Winston reached down and popped another beer open as fast as he could. "You want me to pick you up at 8:00?"

"I will just walk over. It's easier that way. Good night, Winston, I will see you tomorrow night."

"I love you, Gloria."

"I love you too, Winston."

He hung up the phone and started dancing back and forth. "Hey, Herman!" Winston hollered, as he stared at the aquarium. "Can you believe what we just heard?"

Herman just swam about calmly, staring toward Winston with a blank look on his face. He then turned and swam away.

"Can you believe it, Herman?" Winston again asked as he crushed his beer can and made a jump shot for the waste basket. "Two points, Bob Cousy," Winston bragged out loud. "You scorin', little devil, you."

"Come on, Brother Plato," Rodeo Cool yelled as he took a spit in the nearby plant, most of it missing, and landing on the floor. "I can't believe you're not coming."

"Winston, you can't be serious?" Brother Horno the Magnificent asked in dismay. "Hell, I wouldn't miss this beer bust, even if a nymphomaniac that owned a chain of liquor stores showed up."

"Sorry, guys, I've got to do some serious planning," Winston apologized. "You all have fun, down a couple of beers for me."

The rowdy group piled out of the fraternity house, whooping and hollering as they left.

"You'll be sorry, Brother Plato," Rodeo Cool hollered back as he hopped into Brother Sabotage's Chrysler.

Winston watched the caravan drive off, shutting the front door. Then he checked the time on his watch. "Hey, Curiosity," Winston said to the house cat that had approached him and now rubbed on his legs back and forth. "You little Siamese spoiled brat, Gloria is going to be here in ten minutes." Winston reached down and scratched Curiosity's left ear and stroked the cat's chin.

"I expect you to be on your best behavior," Winston warned. "And don't pay any attention to Hansel and Gretel." Winston referred to the two Huskies, that were locked up in the laundry room. "You let them be, understand?"

Curiosity just meowed and sauntered off toward the kitchen to check out the situation behind the laundry room's door and that really set the Husky's off. "Stop barking, damn it," Winston instructed, as he walked into the kitchen and grabbed two large rawhide bones. He opened the door and pitched them at Hansel and Gretel. "There, that ought to keep you busy for awhile," Winston closed the door, "You all be good doggies."

Winston then placed the small latch on the swinging door, locking it. Curiosity watched with intense interest as she hopped up on the cabinet next to the laundry door. Winston ran upstairs to his bathroom to brush his teeth and comb his hair. Afterwards, he splashed a few drops of English Leather cologne on, then scrutinized himself in the mirror. "Perfection," Winston commented, "You good lookin' devil, you."

Winston hurried down the stairs to meet Gloria, who as expected was exactly on time. Opening the door, he motioned her inside, "Good evening, my fair beautiful maiden." Winston guided Gloria up the stairs.

"Where did you get that beautiful dress?" Winston asked as he stared at her yellow silk paisley dress, also taking note that she was not wearing a bra.

"I bought it today," Gloria answered smiling coyly at Winston as she walked up the stairs, slightly in front of him

"You look ravishing, my lady," Winston smiled with approval.

"Cut it out, Winston," Gloria ordered, "You're embarrassing me."

Winston guided Gloria into his room, flipping on the large black light above. The room glowed in blue and the psychedelic posters that hung on the walls also glowed their eerie beauty. Winston walked over to the 8-track player, plugged in Santana and then lit the logs in the fireplace.

"Nice pad," Gloria admired as she looked about the room and at the aquarium behind his bed. "You're the only one I know that has a wood burning fireplace in his fraternity room."

"Only the best for the best," Winston said as he popped open a bottle of champagne.

"Dom Perignon?" Gloria asked in amazement. "You know how expensive this is?"

"Only the best for the best," Winston answered as he poured the champagne into two fine crystal glasses.

"Shall we toast?" Winston asked as he stared directly into Gloria' eyes.

"Sure."

"Here's to my lovely fair maiden," Winston toasted her glass as he sipped from his.

"Winston, it's getting smoky in here, honey, did you open the flue all the way?"

"Damn it," Winston moaned as he walked over and opened the flue, and then to the balcony's adjoining doors, opening them slightly. For the next hour, the pair visited as they sipped their champagne and nibbled on cheese and fruit.

"Gloria, I've been thinking," Winston pondered as he put his glass down by the bedside table.

"Yes?" Gloria asked with interest.

"You're right," Winston nodded. "It's time for me to change my ways. It's time for me to grow up."

"Is that why you skipped the beer bust?" Gloria asked curiously.

Winston didn't answer, just lit the vanilla candle on the bedside table, and guided Gloria down on the bed beside him. The fire burned a soft red glow, but was no match for the light that the black light produced above.

"Black Magic Woman," Gloria smiled her approval at the song that started playing, as she snuggled closer to Winston.

"Your eyes are glowing, Gloria," Winston observed as he brushed her hair back from the right side of her face.

"Black lights are so weird," Gloria replied. "Wonderful music." She reached over and kissed him on the lips, "You're not trying to take advantage of me, are you?"

"Yes, I am," he took her champagne glass from her hand, then guiding her back on the feather pillows behind them. Winston gazed into her eyes, and whispered, "I love you."

"I love you, too."

He kissed her hard on the lips, then her cheeks and around her left ear, and then kissed her softly, repeatedly on the back of her neck.

"You're giving me goose bumps," was all Gloria could say as Winston softly caressed her, kissing her again and again. "Kiss me, Winston, kiss me hard." Gloria passively moaned, as Winston noticed her breathing was getting heavier and her legs wrapped tightly around his. Winston, carefully and slowly opened the buttons on her yellow dress, opening them one by one, until he spread the dress apart revealing two beautiful, excited breasts. Gloria sighed with emotion as Winston kissed all around her breasts, but was careful not to touch them.

"You little tease," Gloria smiled as her legs wrapped harder around Winston's, and she dug her fingernails harder on his back, stroking them up and down. Winston continued to unbutton the front of her dress, and then she stood up and threw it down by the bedside. Lying back down, her head resting softly on the feather pillow, she calmly whispered to Winston as she stared into his blue eyes. "Take me, Winston," she moaned with ecstasy, "Oh God, take me."

Winston kissed her softly on the stomach as he slowly pulled down her royal blue panties. Winston could not believe this was happening as he stared at her top tan line that glowed in the darkened room from the black light above. He continued to slowly pull down on her panties.

"Oh, God, Gloria, you are so damn beautiful," he softly whispered as he stared at her tan line below. "I'm about to make love to a Goddess."

"Make love to me, Winston," Gloria begged, "Now."

Downstairs during this time, and totally unconcerned about what was going on upstairs, Curiosity sat on the kitchen counter, her left kept playing with the hook as she listened to the scratching sounds behind the laundry door, and to the occasional whimpers that the dogs would make.

Finally, her efforts were successful as the hook flipped up and released. Seconds later, the two Siberian huskies flew out, flinging the laundry door wide open as it banged against the wall, knocking over several mounted pledge paddles.

Curiosity crouched down low on the kitchen counter, the hair on her back sticking straight up. Instead of fear in her eyes, she showed a 'why did I do this' look on her face, as she watched the two wild dogs dash about below her. Her efforts to hide proved futile as Hansel suddenly discovered her, and jumped wildly against the counter. Curiosity leaped off the counter and on to the breakfast table, with both dogs following in close pursuit. Chairs flew about like broken limbs as the two huskies almost caught Curiosity's tail as she escaped their lunges in the nick of time. Curiosity raced full speed around the kitchen corner into the living area.

Gretel, in her rush to capture the furry prize, slid across the kitchen floor crashing her head into the small wine rack sending bottle crashing and rolling all over the kitchen. Both huskies, their paws now soaked with red wine, continued their wild stampede after their elusive prey. Curiosity in a hopeless attempt to escape her predators jumped up on the fireplace mantle. Both dogs rushed across the room, bolting from the coffee table and crashing into the mantle.

An antique clock that stood proudly on the Kappa house's mantle for over twenty years, tumbled to the floor, breaking up into several pieces. Curiosity sprinted across the living area, at lightning speed as she attempted to escape the duo. She dug her claws hard into the brown drapes that covered the fraternity house's front picture window but the two charging dogs crashed into the window sending the right drape collapsing onto them. Hansel now completely covered by the falling drape, jumped back and forth totally freaked out by his blindness. Lamps, and ashtrays flew everywhere, shattering into pieces as Hansel tried to shake off the drape.

After a few minutes, Hansel shook off the fabric and joined Gretel as she chased the cat up the stairs. The living room was now a wreck covered in broken glass and red paw prints that tracked across the cream colored plush living room carpet. The eight red-stained paws continued to stamp out their ominous path as they followed Curiosity closely up the stairs. Curiosity, after flying up the stairs, turned a screeching right and bolted through Winston's partially open door with the dogs again in close pursuit.

The two lovers were totally oblivious to the rambunctious behavior of the animals that were downstairs. Instead Winston had, with a deliberate slowness, just about removed Gloria's panties. Curiosity now raced through the room flying over the bedside table, hopping over Gloria's head as she made her exit through the slightly opened balcony doors.

"What the f…" Winston raised his head, as he watched the two Siberian huskies kick the door open and rush hysterically into the room after their prey. Before Winston could react, Hansel, in close pursuit of the cat, crashed head long over the bedside coffee table, his right leg pulled the lamp cord with him, as he flung himself wildly on the bed with Gretel following just a foot or two behind. The lamp crashed hard into the aquarium. Glass and water spewed everywhere, as the fish wiggled about in helplessness.

"What the hell is going on, Winston?" Gloria screamed in a hysterical voice, as she rolled off the bed dodging the broken glass, water, and squirming fish as best she could.

The two Siberian huskies dashed off the bed, as they continued their pursuit after their yellow furry prey right out the balcony doors. Winston reached down and picked up Herman and rushed him over to the trash can. Gently lying him carefully inside, he returned to the aquarium and splashed what little water was left into the trash can. Then realizing his mistake, he turned quickly to Gloria.

"Are you okay?" Winston asked as he knelt down beside her, and brushed her wet hair away from her face. "Are you okay?"

Gloria remained silent, as she stood up nearly naked, soaking wet, with small glass cuts all over her arms. Then she reached for her dress, before she realized that it was too wet to put on.

"Damn it, Winston," Gloria screamed out in frustration. "Don't just stand there like an idiot. Do something, even if it's wrong - do something." Gloria put her hands to her face, as she cried in hopelessness, "You have some explaining to do, damn you," Gloria said as she reached for something to put on. "Do you have a robe in this place?"

Winston rushed into the bathroom and returned with a white terrycloth robe, wrapping it around Gloria, he hugged her, "You okay?"

"Sure, Winston, I'm just doing fine," Gloria answered as she stared at the hopeless mess in front of them.

"Winston, damn you," Gloria shook her head in a hopeless gesture. "You care more about that damn fish than you do me."

"That's not true," Winston answered.

"Where did those damn dogs come from?" Gloria asked as she paced back and forth, dodging the small pieces of glass that were below her feet, but her confusion turned to suspicion as she studied the look on Winston's face.

"Well?" She asked again.

"Okay Gloria," Winston hesitated as he proceeded to tell Gloria the entire story.

"Winston, I can't believe you." Gloria shook her head as she walked in front of the fireplace, and stared almost trance-like at the burning fire. "Winston, you lied to me," Gloria shook her head again in frustration. "You're never going to change." Tears streamed down her cheeks as she lectured Winston, "This was all a dog and pony show, wasn't it, Brother Plato?" Gloria asked Winston, raising her voice, "You did all of this just to fuck me." Gloria backed off from his apologetic advance. "Just leave me alone, Winston, I can't believe I said that word. Just leave me alone."

"Gloria, I'm sorry, I'm truly sorry," Winston attempted to sooth her. "And I really do love you."

"Winston, it's over, you're never going to change, and you're just going to waste away with all your worthless buddies. You might as well join a carnival show at least that way you all would fit in." Gloria threw her hands up in the air, "Please find me some dry clothes, I want to go home." Gloria put on the gray jogging suit that he handed her, and walked toward the door. "I give up, Winston. When and if you can prove to me that you have changed your life," Gloria walked out into the hallway as she headed for the stairs, "then give me a call."

Winston watched her hurry down the stairs and shut the front door hard behind her then he went back in his room and reached for a beer out of the cooler.

You dumb shit, you blew it, Winston moaned in total disgust. *Just seconds away, and those Goddamn dogs screw it up.* Winston kicked the metal cooler with his foot. *I've lost Gloria. It's all Sgt. T.'s fault with his lame-brain scheme.*

Winston lit a cigarette and stared at the broken aquarium. "Herman, we need to find you and your friends a new home." He looked around at all the broken glass on the bed, and his thoughts refocused on Gloria. Winston shrugged, "Sometimes you just gotta blow that shit off, Herman." Winston took a sip of beer and then plugged in a tape by the Beatles.

"Yesterday, all my troubles seemed so far away…"

Chapter

Ten

Winston sat in his usual chair at the Kappa Kappa table in the Student Union Building playing spades with Rodeo Cool, and Brother Horno the Magnificent. It was nearly ten a.m. on Monday morning after the 'Great Escape' episode.

"Hey, Winston, if you don't get moving, you're gonna miss your ten o'clock," Rodeo Cool warned as he fiddled with his cards, occasionally spitting chewing tobacco juice in the plastic cup that he kept between his legs. Most of the time he was accurate, but every so often, the spit would hit his jeans, or drip on his shirt instead of hitting the plastic cup.

"You're a slob, Rodeo Cool," Brother Horno blurted out as he stared at Rodeo Cool's tobacco-stained shirt.

"Why don't you go fu…" Rodeo started.

"All right, all right, knock it off!" Winston ordered, as he turned around to Sgt. T., who was sitting next to Winston, dressed in his usual army field jacket, and wearing his 'Lennon look alike' sunglasses. "The natives are getting restless John, and their tempers are getting short."

"I know," Sgt. T. answered, as he lit up a cigarette.

"The General's Ball is less than five weeks away," Winston said as he drew a card from the deck, "and we don't have a damn dime in our social fund."

"I know, man," Sgt. T. agreed. "Winston its ten o'clock, you need to hoof it, you're late."

"Oh, to hell with Kelly's government class," Winston answered, as he lit up a cigarette. "Too damn boring, and besides we have to figure out some way to raise enough money to have our General's Ball," Winston paused to blow a few smoke rings up into the air, "or we won't pledge a soul next spring."

"Oh, shit," Brother Horno moaned as he watched Michael Gentile and Laura Love move toward the Kappa table.

"Well, if it isn't Arnie Palmer," Michael smirked, "seen any cute doggies lately?"

Winston knew that there were no secrets kept in this town. Gossip spread like a West Texas wildfire.

"You gonna have a backyard barbeque for this year's General Ball, Winston?" Michael asked in his cocky Italian accent. "Whose gonna be the band, the famous Music Man?"

Winston sat quietly unable to come back with a jab.

"And guess who's coming to the Delta's White Rose Formal?" Laura asked as she held Michael's left arm tightly.

"And who might that be?" Winston asked as he blew smoke from his cigarette toward her face.

"The one and only, Rocco Orlando, and his girlfriend Destiny."

"Yea, that's right, cowboys," Michael again smirked. "Eat your heart out."

Winston again didn't answer, just took another drag off his cigarette.

"Good luck in spring rush next year, Brother Plato," Michael offered. "Sure hope the Kappas have a lot of legacies enrolling."

"They're laughing at us again," Brother Horno groaned, "we're going to. . ." but before he could finish his thought, he was distracted by a tall blond that walked by their table. "Damn, who the hell is she? Check those wheels out," Horno stared in his usual stupor. "My God, they would get tangled up in a ceiling fan."

"Down boy," Winston grinned.

"Can you believe it?" Brother Beerwolf asked as he approached the table, watching Michael and Laura walk away. "The number one box office male stud muffin, who has three top motion pictures out this year, and his knockout model girlfriend, Destiny, are going to be at the Delta White Rose Formal."

Brother Beerwolf growled, "And here we are, with not a dime to our name," Beerwolf shook his head back and forth. "Peace Corps anybody?"

"Damn it," Sgt. T. griped, "we're becoming the laughing stock of the entire University."

"How did Michael get Rocco to come here?" Rodeo Cool asked.

"They grew up together back in Brooklyn," Brother Pens answered, "even heard that Michael saved his life when they were in grade school together."

Winston again remained silent, as he puffed on his cigarette. "Confidence, my Brothers," Winston assured as he calmly flipped his discard toward the middle of the table. "I will come up with a solution, I always have," Winston put out his cigarette and stood up and stretched. "So we are zero for two in our best laid plans to raise money." Winston walked toward the door. "I say the third time's a charm." With that final thought, Winston left them.

"Yeah, well what's that third charm gonna be?" Rodeo Cool asked as he tried to remove the brown stains on his shirt with a soda soaked napkin.

Chapter

Eleven

"All right, Brothers, the executive council is now in session," Winston ordered as he popped open a bottle of beer. "As we are all aware," Winston continued, "The General's Ball is less than a month away, and we have only $300 in our social fund," Winston paused to light a cigarette, "And that my Brothers is $3,700 short." Winston stopped and looked at the members seated around the table. "Well, anyone got any bright ideas?"

The members before him remained silent, even Billy The Kid had nothing to offer.

Finally Sgt. T. spoke, "Brother Plato , what's your plan?"

Winston took a deep drag from his cigarette, blowing the smoke out slowly, he proceeded, "There's a small house that's up for sale in the historic Highland Park Gardens, just a block from ol' man Howell's estate."

"So?" Brother Sabotage asked skeptically, "What are we going to do, sell it?"

Brother Dancin' Beerwolf laughed out loud.

"All right, knock it off with the smart remarks," Winston ordered, "This is serious shit."

"You're right, Brother Plato," Beerwolf apologized, "Sorry about that."

"No we are not going to sell it," Winston paused to sip on his beer as he looked at the Brothers' curious expressions, "We are going to buy it."

"Winston," Sgt. T. shook his head sadly, "You need to slow up on those beers, man. You're starting to lose it."

"How much are they asking for the house?" Manse calmly asked.

"$90,000," Winston answered without blinking an eye.

"Winston, you gotta be kidding," said Billy.

"Brothers, it's quite simple," Winston grinned as he sipped on his beer. "We purchase the house," Pointing his finger at Brother Beerwolf he continued, "And you, Brother Beerwolf, and Roll 'em Rick are going to live there - at least temporarily."

"What are you gettin' at?" Charlie The Spoon Luna asked with a confused look.

"It's quite simple," Winston smiled sarcastically. "You two move in, and within days you will watch your snobby neighbors go into hysterics. You talk about a neighborhood going to hell," Winston paused to chuckle.

"I still don't get it," Charlie Luna shook his head.

"Charlie, we're going to look so bad as neighbors that we will force them to buy us out - just to get rid of us."

Billy The Kid laughed, "Brother Plato, you're a genius, no wonder we elected you Prez."

"Still don't get it," Charlie again mumbled.

"Charlie, Beerwolf, and Roll'em are going to gross their neighbors out so badly that they will buy 'em out, just to get rid of them," Winston paused to grin, "And our asking price will be $100,000, and not one penny less."

Manse listened carefully to the discussion, before finally offering his usual cautious advice. "All fine and dandy, Winston," Manse warned, "but Highland Park Gardens has major restrictions that are strictly enforced."

"I appreciate your concerns, Brother Pens," Winston answered confidently, "but I've all ready done my homework on this matter." Winston stopped to pullout a manila folder. "Here are all the deed and property restrictions and I have reviewed them carefully. The house will look as it should, and the yard will look immaculate as required."

"So?" Charlie asked, "How are we going to pull this off?"

"Brothers, visualize a picture if you will," Winston paused for effect. "It's a sunny October Sunday afternoon, and we have Brother Beerwolf sitting on the front porch in his undershirt wearing an Indian headband, beside him his Brother Roll'em Rick decked out in his black leather Harley outfit with his bike parked nearby and Rodeo Cool is sittin' in a cheap plastic chair spittin' chewing tobacco in a mayonnaise jar." Winston laughed, "And in front of them is a washtub full of iced down beer and Boone's Farm wine." Winston sipped his beer, "Now do we start to get the picture?"

"I'm starting to catch on," Charlie answered smiling.

"And," Winston continued, "how about a nice clothesline on the side of the house with Beerwolf's and Roll'em's clothes hanging on it?" Winston grinned, "Maybe a few bras and panties hanging on it too."

"A clothesline?" Manse asked suspiciously. "No way you can get away with that."

"Oh, yes we can," Winston fired back. "There is no regulation or restriction preventing it," Winston said. "Hell, no one would ever have thought it would have been needed."

"You're on a roll," Charlie congratulated. "However, Brother Plato, where are we going to get the down payment?"

"I'm glad you asked that, Brother Spoon," Winston answered with a devilish grin. "And that is where you come in."

Charlie stood up with a panicked look in his eyes. "Oh, no, Winston, not this time," Charlie blurted out with a concerned voice. "My parents have cut me off, other than the bare necessities and besides I've lost a fortune to all you guys' crazy ideas." Charlie paused to point his finger at Brother Billy. Sobering up quickly, Charlie set his Boone's Farm apple wine bottle down, and continued, "Remember, Brother Kid, the lock we had on the Cowboys and Redskins game last fall?"

Billy managed to mumble a sheepish, "Yes."

"Remember, no way we can lose, you said it's rigged, that you had an inside tip from one of the biggest bookies in the country."

Billy dipped his head low, but did not answer.

Charlie continued, "That clever tip cost me my $2,500 boat."

Charlie stopped, nervously taking a swig of wine. "And Billy, what about last spring when I backed you in the big pool shootout with that Oriental kid from Frisco? Pigeon city, as I remember what you said." Charlie shook his head, "That cost me $1,400." Charlie turned to Winston, "No way, Winston, and besides, I ain't got no bread to loan you, even if I could."

"Charlie, I have all ready arranged for a $10,000 loan from our Alumni banker, Mainess Harris. "That's how much he will loan us on your 1968 Corvette that is fully paid for."

"No, Winston, you can't do this to me," Charlie pleaded.

Winston, trying to calm down Charlie's fears, continued in a low calm voice. "Brother Spoon, we are not asking you to sell it, all we want to do is use it for collateral for a 30 day note." Winston stared at Charlie with his puppy dog begging look. "All I'm asking is for a 30 day loan, you'll clear $1,000 for yourself after we sell the house." Winston snapped his fingers, "just like that! It's a shoo-in, Charlie, no way we can lose on this one."

"No, Winston," Charlie answered, "You're not going to sucker me in this time."

"Please, Charlie, it's for the future of the Kappa Kappas," Winston begged.

"Please, Winston," Charlie pleaded again.

"Charlie, you're our last chance," Winston leaned on Charlie's conscience, "if you say no, there will be no General's Ball, not only that, our chapter will be history."

Charlie sat back down in his chair, and remained silent for a few seconds, before finally speaking. "Oh, all right," Charlie reluctantly agreed. "But it better work, or I'm going to be disinherited, and I'm not kidding."

"Way to go, Charlie," Brother Beerwolf cheered. "That's the Kappa Kappa spirit."

"Meeting adjourned," Winston announced pounding the gavel on the table. "Let's all stand and give Charlie a toast, our man of the hour."

Chapter

Twelve

Winston drove his 1966 blue Cutlass through the Highland Park Garden's open iron gates, and continued past the towering iron statue of Charles Goodnight, a famous legendary figure in panhandle history. Around the statue were seven bronze longhorn cattle that always were wet from the water from the shooting fountains. Winston reflected on how he and Gloria would ride up and down this historic district every Sunday afternoon, admiring the beautiful homes and learning who the families were that lived in them.

"Damn it," Winston moaned. "Sure wish Gloria was with me." He continued down Goodnight Avenue which contained the biggest estates in the Garden area. Winston looked over to his right at his favorite house, a beautiful white colonial house with tall white columns, built in 1929 by the biggest cattle baron in Texas at the time, R.D. Williamson. The mansion was built on a two acre plot, and was one of the few homes that had a horse stable.

Winston turned off Goodnight Avenue and onto Churchill Street, whose overhanging huge elm trees were the first planted in the neighborhood, and it was also the first block in Amarillo to lay brick streets. The homes, although much older and smaller compared to the rest of the estates in the area, were still very quaint and charming, particularly the two story stucco house, named "The Wisteria House" for all its beautiful purple flowers that bloomed in the springtime, and dangled off the stucco front wall. Winston lit a cigarette and smiled as he drove into the stucco house's driveway, parking his car behind Brother Beerwolf's 1954 white Packard. He joined the trio hanging out on the front porch.

"Bet your neighbors love those rusted out back fenders, Brother Beerwolf," Winston hollered as he walked up the stone steps, "and when are you going to get that flat fixed?"

Beerwolf smiled, "Welcome to Poodle City, Brother Plato."

"What's happenin', dude," was all Roll'em Rick could manage to mutter, as he sat nearby, decked out in Harley gear.

Beerwolf reached into the bucket and handed Winston a cold beer. "If I knew you were coming on this lovely sunny Sunday afternoon, I would have looked more presentable. Please excuse my dirty white undershirt and turquoise headband."

Winston just smiled, took a sip from his beer and looked over at Rodeo Cool who was quietly rocking back and forth in his cheap plastic chair, spittin' tobacco juice into his mayonnaise jar. Winston laughed as he looked at the lumberjack western looking outfit that Rodeo was wearing.

"My God, Rodeo," Winston laughed, "That cowboy hat

you got on has more sweat stains than a football jersey after a hot summer practice." Winston shook his head. "What did you do, wear that hat while you took a sauna?"

Rodeo didn't answer but rubbed on his red handlebar mustache, and wiped the tobacco juice off the left side with his left sleeve. "Like our new pad?"

"We're just startin' to get used to the place after two and a half weeks." Beerwolf commented as he pulled out a beer out of the washtub and started rubbing on the big mixed breed dog that lay beside him. "Like Spot, our Heinz 57 dog that we rescued from the animal shelter?" Beerwolf let out a loud Indian holler, and started laughing, "Man, Brother Plato, you ought to see the glares we get when we take spot for a walk. These inheritees ain't never seen a mongrel dog before."

Winston smiled and motioned to the twinkle lights dangling precariously from the eaves. "I drove by here last night, and noticed you all are the only ones in the neighborhood with Christmas lights; it's only the second day after Halloween, you know."

"We thought we would get an early start," Beerwolf answered.

Winston smiled, "And I must congratulate you all, they are the ugliest light display I think I have ever had the privilege of observing. They are so wonderfully crooked and out of place. It looks like W.C. Fields hung them while on a bender."

"Thanks a lot, dude," Roll'em mumbled.

Winston grinned, "And what's with orange and pink lights for Christmas?"

"We did the best we could, man," Rodeo sarcastically answered as he accidentally knocked over the jar under his chair, spilling black juice all over the stone porch. "Shit."

"It's been interesting, Winston," Beerwolf commented.

"They have been conducting emergency meetings almost every day to pass new restrictions. First, we had to take down our clothesline."

"What a fuckin' bummer, man," Roll'em interrupted.

Beerwolf agreed. "Then we had to pull up all our plastic pink flamingos - those were the first two restrictions that they nailed us with," Beerwolf stopped to shake his head sadly.

"There have been 14 others passed also. Brother Plato, they're really picking on us."

"You ought to see the dirty looks we get, when our neighbors walk by our house." Rodeo laughed as he started coughing up juice, "Damn it, I'm choking again."

"Winston, you should have been here the first day when we unloaded our furniture - all nine pickup loads," Beerwolf paused and started laughing, "$78 worth of the finest furniture that you can buy at the Salvation Army. You should have seen their faces when we unloaded all that crap."

"Hey, dude, I liked some of that crap," Roll'em interrupted.

Beerwolf just smiled as he popped open another beer, "But our plan is working, Winston, Ol' Judge Parker that lives over there across the street in that French lookin' house, called us this morning. He wants to meet with us tomorrow afternoon."

"What for?" Winston asked excitedly.

"Word is that he wants to make an offer on our house so his newly married daughter can move in."

"Yeah, man, we've spotted the snoopin' bitch peeking in our window when we drove up the other day," Rodeo reported to Winston as he pulled a Boone's Farm bottle out of the ice.

Winston lit a cigarette, smiled and then his mood turned serious. "Good, because we are running out of time. We can't afford to let this drag on."

"No sweat, Sherlock," Beerwolf confidently answered. "Roll'em Rick's Harley ridin' dudes are going to join us in about an hour, that ought to put the icing on the cake."

Later on, Winston sat on his bed staring at Herman's new fish tank. "Well, Herman, it's 11:00. Think I ought to call Gloria up?" Winston stared at Herman as he lit a cigarette and watched Herman's tail wiggle back and forth. "I guess that means yes."

Popping open a beer, Winston struck up enough nerve to call Gloria, whom he hadn't seen or talked to since the dog fiasco three weeks earlier.

"Hello?" Gloria quietly answered.

"Hi. Gloria," Winston's palms sweated, "How are things going?" He waited for an answer, but Gloria remained silent.

"Gloria, you okay?" Winston asked.

"Winston, don't call me anymore, please," she said. "Good night."

The dial toned hummed in his ear. Winston sat for a while in near darkness, puffing heavily on his cigarette, "Well, Herman, I think I blew it." Winston tapped his finger on the tank as he stared at the fish and managed a weak smile. "You know what they say in the ol' country, don't you? When in doubt, you just gotta blow that shit off."

He reached down and pulled a beer out of the ice chest. "And besides, Herman, there's a knockout Polynesian girl that has been giving me the eye lately when she passes by our table in the Student Union. Her name is Desiree and is she beautiful. You ought to see her, Herman. She's as tall as I am, with a fabulous light brown complexion and long black straight hair not to mention those wide exotic lips, and long brown perfectly shaped legs."

Winston paused to sip on his beer, "Gotta quit talking about her Herman, it's driving me crazy."

Chapter Thirteen

"Can you believe it, Sgt. T.?" Winston gloated. "$10,000 profit in 24 days." He slapped his hand down on the Kappa table. "After $1,000 to Charlie, and after closing fees, the chapter cleared over $8,000."

Sgt. T., sitting on Winston's left wearing his usual Lennon-like glasses smiled. "Boy, was Judge Parker a hot one when we were at the title office. I think if he had a gun he would have shot Brother Dancin' Beerwolf who couldn't keep from smirkin' through the whole meeting."

"Oh, screw him," Winston said. "$10,000 is a mere drop in the bucket for him compared to all the gas wells and ranch land that he has inherited." Winston turned to his right and patted Desiree's shoulder, "And Brothers, my lovely girlfriend, Desiree, has never been to a General's Ball before, and we want to be damn sure that it will be the best one ever."

Desiree said nothing, just smiled, her beautiful white teeth glowing like pearls.

Winston continued, "We are going to put the Delta Phi's White Rose to shame. Even the Eta Zeta's have been warmin' up to us this week, since they found out who the band was that we are bringing in from Las Vegas."

"What band, dude?" Roll'em Rick asked.

"Haven't you heard, Rick," Beerwolf asked, "Mr. Soul has got us the best show band in Las Vegas to play at the General's Ball - Johnny Flash and the Jumpin' Jacks."

"They do perfect impersonations of the Rolling Stones and the Beatles," Winston added, "They cost us $1,500, but it will be worth every penny, just to hear the talk around campus." Winston smiled, then asked, "Can you believe it, a ten piece celebrity show band playing at our ball?"

"Now's your chance to meet our arch rival, Desiree." Winston grinned and calmly lit a cigarette as he watched Michael and Laura walk through the doorway and head for their table.

"Starting to smell like a feedyard around here," Rodeo Cool spoke loud enough for Michael to hear as he approached the Kappa Kappa table.

Michael struck a pose in his usual cocky manner, wearing black jeans and a tight fitting white shirt. Laura looking as beautiful as ever, stood beside Michael, and brushed her blond hair back repeatedly.

"Good morning, cowboys," Michael smirked, "Let's see now - kidnapping, extortion, and blackmail - must be you guys new motto. Tank, when he returns from Vietnam, is gonna be really proud of you guys."

"Eat your heart out, Michael," Winston answered.

"Have fun at your little ball, cowboys, if you have one," Michael smirked as he started walking away, "and if you guys are good little cowboys, I'll get Rocco Orlando and Destiny to give you a few autographs."

"He's up to something," Winston stared across the table at Brother Sabotage.

"You're right, Winston," Sabotage agreed, "and we better be on guard."

"I don't understand, Winston," Desiree asked in a soft voice with a puzzled expression on her face.

"Desiree, there's always a little game that the Kappas and Deltas play against each other. We're all trying to figure out clever ways to screw up each other's planned events."

"Why, honey?" Desiree asked frowning.

"Why not?" Winston answered, "It started awhile back when they ruined our calf fry fundraiser at the big Gene Autry Arena instead of raising $2,100, it cost our chapter $1,100."

"Winston, what are calf fries?"

"Oh, Desiree, I keep forgetting that you have only been in Texas for just a few months," Winston laughed.

"Well, every year we have a big cook off with a big band, and the main dish is," Winston hesitated, "Well, fried bull testicles, which are known in the Texas Panhandle as calf fries."

"Winston, how disgusting," Desiree shook her head in shock.

"Anyway," Winston continued, "two of the cooks hired to fix all those calf fries were Delta plants." Winston grimaced. "It must have taken them hours the night before to surgically remove the cooked meat and replace them with uncooked testicles, and mixing them in with the cooked ones."

"My God, Winston, you're making me sick." Desiree's face turned color-from light brown to almost pale white.

"Sorry, honey," Winston held her left hand. "Anyhow, it was awful. Girls were biting into supposedly cooked fries, only to find uncooked ones squirting out. Girls were screaming and throwing up everywhere." Winston shook his head and then smiled, "You have to admire those bastards, they pulled off a good one, damn near got us sued."

"How gross, Winston," Desiree frowned.

"Desiree, we got 'em good at their Spring Fling party," Brother Beerwolf volunteered, "Brother Sabotage rigged up the sprinkler system at the Hilton ballroom to go off right in the middle of the awards presentation."

"It took nearly 20 minutes before the maintenance guys showed up," Horno the Magnificent laughed as he patted Desiree's right shoulder, "completely shut down the party." Horno laughed again, "Damn it, I wish I was there come to think of it."

"How's that?" Beerwolf asked curiously.

"Just think," Horno reflected. "With all those girls runnin' about braless with all their blouses soaking wet, a regular wet t-shirt contest in the making."

"Down boy," Winston ordered, "down boy."

"All right, Sgt. T. and Brother Sabotage," Winston's mood turned serious, "We have to be on red alert. We can't take a chance on the Deltas pulling off some stunt to screw up our General's ball. After all, we will have over $4,000 invested in this party," Winston paused to light up a cigarette, "and we have got to kick their asses with the best party if we are going to do good in rush this coming spring."

"No sweat, Sherlock," Brother Sabotage promised, "we'll have so much preparation and security at the Harvey Hotel, that the Viet Cong couldn't even get through." Sabotage stopped as he showed a sadistic smile. "I've got several of my special forces buddies comin' to town for that weekend. If the Deltas try anything, they will be dead meat."

Chapter

Fourteen

The beautiful Harvey Hotel's huge circular ballroom was the perfect setting for the General's Ball that was now well on its way on this Friday night. Every flag possible dangled from the rafters above, cavalry flags, American flags, military banners, you name it - they hung above the masquerade gathering below them. Every conceivable famous General of American and European history was represented. The Music Man all dressed up in his Napoleon outfit, Brother Billy The Kid, all decked out as General George Custer with his cavalry hat, sword, and long curly blond hair that hung down way below his neck. It was truly a sight to behold watching five star Generals, and famous legendary heroes dance wildly to the blaring rock music that blasted out from the stage.

"Can you believe it, Desiree," Winston smiled with delight,

"Johnny Flash and the Jumpin' Jacks are better than I ever thought they could be," Winston stopped to pour a beer from the pitcher that was in front of him.

"My dear, George Washington," Desiree smiled as she kissed Winston on his lips and ran her fingers through his white curly locks. "Love your sexy locks, and that sexy uniform you're wearing, but what's Martha going to say when she finds out about us?"

Winston just smiled as he watched Sgt. T. approach the table decked out in his Captain John Smith costume, accompanied by his tall oriental girlfriend, who was wearing a deerskin dress and a turquoise head band with one feather standing up.

"Hey, General Washington," Sgt. T. hollered out loudly over the blaring music, "Have you met Pocahontas yet?"

Winston stood up and bowed his head, "Good evening, my dear Indian Princess." He then turned to Sgt. T., "I didn't know John Smith was a General."

"Close enough, man," Sgt. T. answered as they watched Charlie The Spoon Luna and Dancin' Beerwolf approach the table.

Observing their costumes, Winston yelled, "I didn't know Davy Crockett and Sittin' Bull were buddies."

"Learn something every day, don't you George?" Beerwolf answered.

"What a hell of a party," Beerwolf did a quick Indian dance as he let out a loud war cry.

"So far, so good," Winston calmly stated as he lit up a cigar, "and look who just walked up?" He pointed toward Roll'em Rick, who as usual wore his black leather outfit, and dark sunglasses.

"And who might you be, Brother Rick?" Winston asked cynically.

"Call my ass, General Dude, man," Roll'em replied as he poured a beer from the table pitcher. The Rolling Stones song *Brown Sugar* sounded in the background, as everybody from the table stood up to head for the dance floor.

"Let's dance, Desiree," Winston guided her toward the dance floor.

Dancing to *Brown Sugar*, then to *Jumpin' Jack Flash*, and then to *Honky Tonk Woman*. Winston and Desiree finally took a break, returning to their table.

"Damn, they're good," Winston praised as he poured another beer. "Not only do they sound like the stones, they look like them. Johnny Flash looks like Mick Jagger's twin Brother, and his moves copy Mick's to perfection."

Rodeo Cool slowly strolled toward their table.

"Well, if it isn't Buffalo Bill himself," Winston commented as he looked over Rodeo's western outfit, in particular Buffalo Bill's trademark hat that he was wearing.

"Hey, Buffalo Bill," Beerwolf hollered, "how's the scouting going this fall? Trackin' down any redskins?"

Rodeo did not reply just rubbed on his handlebar mustache. "Don't get cocky," Rodeo warned, "I can handle any bull including you."

"Watch it, paleface," Beerwolf warned, "how would you like a tomahawk shoved up your ass?"

"All right, Brothers," Winston laughed, "remember the treaty." Winston's smile changed to a frown as he watched Brother Pens rush toward their table, with Brother Horno following close behind.

"What's wrong, General Robert E. Lee?" Winston asked staring at Manse's confederate uniform and silver beard. "And who the hell is that French general that is following you?"

"No time for jokes, Brother Plato," Manse warned, "We have two Liquor Control Board guys standing over there next to the stage, and they want to talk to you."

Winston quickly rose up from his chair and followed Manse over to the two men.

"Good evening, gentlemen," Winston greeted them, "and what can I do for you?"

"Good evening, Winston," the taller officer answered, "I'm Lt. Bill Harrington with the Amarillo Liquor Control Board, and this is Sgt. Will Bentley."

Winston nodded. *Damn they look familiar..*

Lt. Harrington continued, "Winston, we are here to inform you that there is alcohol that is being served to minors at this party, and that is illegal, and we simply cannot allow this to continue."

Winston couldn't believe what he had just heard. "Sir, in all due respect, we've had our General's Ball at this private establishment for the last nine years. This is a private party on private property, Lieutenant you have no jurisdiction here."

Lt. Harrington just smiled and then continued, "That's incorrect, as of last Thursday we do."

Winston with a puzzled look on his face questioned his authority. "And just how is that?" Winston asked sarcastically.

"If you had read the local papers lately, Winston, you would have known that this hotel has been turned over to the city for back taxes," Lt. Harrington paused and then continued, "and until all the attorneys for each party can reach a compromise, this hotel is temporarily under the City of Amarillo's control."

"You gotta be kidding me," Winston retorted.

"No, we are not," Lt. Harrington answered seriously.

"Consider yourself lucky. If we wanted to, we could haul half of you in for minor in possession charges and public intoxication on city property," Lt. Harrington stopped as he cynically smiled, obviously pleased with his power. "Instead, we are going to do you all a favor this time. I want this party ended now. You have fifteen minutes to vacate this hotel, or we will change our minds."

"But please, we have $4,000 invested in this party, and the award ceremonies are about to begin," Winston pleaded.

"Sorry, Winston," Lt. Harrington apologized, "we're only doing our job. You can blame the hotel for this fiasco. If they had paid their city taxes, you all wouldn't be in this fix."

"Damn, " Winston muttered.

"Now, gentlemen, you have fifteen minutes to clear this place out, so I suggest you get moving."

Winston turned quickly away and walked toward the stage.

Sgt. T. ran up to Winston, "What the hell is going on?"

"The L.C.B.'s are here, and they have informed us that we have to vacate these premises in fifteen minutes, or they will start making arrests."

"They ain't got the authority to do that," Brother Sabotage blurted out with a glaring look in his eyes toward the two men.

"Yeah, they do," Winston answered. "I don't have time to explain, I've got to make a quick announcement."

"You want Sgt. T. and me to take care of these jerks?" Brother Sabotage asked with a gleam in his eyes.

"Forget it," Winston warned, "They got us by the balls."

Winston walked onto the stage and approached one of the microphones.

"Sing us a lullaby, Brother Plato," one of the Kappas hollered out.

"Hey, Brother Plato, how about a few words of wisdom?" Horno the Magnificent shouted out as he raised his drink high in the air.

"All right, Kappa Kappas, hold it down and listen carefully," Winston ordered. "Those two men standing over there are with the Amarillo Liquor Control Board, and they have ordered us to clear out now." Winston paused for a second and continued, "And I mean now. Move it or they will start making arrests."

Boos and loud shouts scattered through the crowd.

"No way, man," Roll em'Rick hollered, "these dudes can't do this shit."

"Now everybody clear out, the party is over," Winston yelled, "and that is an order."

Members and their dates started scattering toward the two exits, as they mumbled and groaned their disappointment.

Johnny Flash walked over to Winston. "Sorry, Winston," Johnny offered his condolence.

"Could have been a great party, Johnny," Winston sighed, "the best we've ever had." Winston walked off the stage as the ten piece band began to break down their equipment. He went over to the table and took Desiree's hand, "Let's get out of here, honey. This is too much for me to take."

"Sorry, Winston."

"Oh, what the hell," Winston answered as he headed toward the side exit, "We will just have to blow this shit off."

The couple exited the building and walked through the parking lot. Horno, Sabotage, Beerwolf, Sgt. T. and their dates followed the two along with several other couples.

"Slow down, Winston," Desiree begged, "I can't walk in

this snow that fast in these stupid shoes."

"I'm sorry, Desiree," Winston slowed down his pace.

"Where are we going, Brother Plato?" Horno asked as he approached Winston.

"We're going across the street, over there to the Cattlemen's Club. I need a stiff drink ,and it ain't gonna be beer."

"All right," Horno excitedly replied, "that chick, Sue Ella, works there, and she got the best set of…"

"Down, Horno," Winston ordered, "Down boy."

"We're going to get laughed out of that cowboy joint in these costumes, Winston," Sgt. T. warned.

"Screw 'em if they can't take a joke," Winston answered, "Damn snow, I'm freezing my ass off." Winston smiled, "How the hell did George Washington cross the Delaware without freezin' to death?"

The large group crossed Amarillo Boulevard, which was once a busy cross country highway called Route 66, before the interstate highway was built not too far away.

Winston stopped, "Something is rotten in Denmark, Brothers."

"What do you mean?" Brother Sabotage asked.

"Look over there," Winston pointed his finger at the side parking area, "do you see what I see?"

"Hey, dude," Roll'em Rick just shook his head, "this dude don't see nothin' but a bunch of fuckin' white snow."

"Look over there, Brothers," Winston again instructed pointing with his right hand, "look at that white truck. Damn it, I knew I've seen that Lt. Harrington before."

Sgt. T. laughed, "Oh, hell, Winston, he's probably busted you before."

"Look what the side of that truck says." Winston pointed again. The sign read, Zip Dog - Have Practical Joke, Will Travel.

"You lost me, Winston," Brother Spoon mumbled.

Winston threw his cigarette down in disgust, "Brothers, we've been had by the Deltas, those sons of a bitch."

"What are you talking about, Brother Plato?" Dancin' Beerwolf asked as he pulled on his braided hair.

"That was a dog and pony show back there, carried out by Zip Dog. That Lt. Harrington back there was Slim Jim with a fake badge." Winston kicked the snow in frustration, "I knew I had seen that son of a bitch before. Damn it, I should have recognized him. They make a living pulling off practical jokes."

"So what do we do now?" Brother Sabotage asked.

"All right, Brothers, let's roll," Winston instructed, "and I mean fast. Beerwolf haul ass back to the ballroom and tell Johnny that the party is fixin' to start back. Everybody spread out and tell any of our Brothers that haven't left, to get back to the ballroom." Winston pointed to one of their young pledges, "Hey, Pledge Mills, go into the Cattlemen's Club and call all the usual Kappa bar hangouts, and tell them to get back here pronto."

"Yes sir, Mr. Fox."

"Brother Sabotage, you have flares in your car?" Winston asked.

"You think I'm stupid, or something?" Sabotage asked grinning. "Of course, I do."

"Then let's get to your car and shoot them," Winston ordered. "You remember the Kappa Kappa distress signal, don't you?"

"Two quick flares, with one following a few seconds later."

Two minutes later, Winston watched the first two red flares shoot up into the air, with the third soon following.

"That should do it," Winston commented. "All right, Brothers, it's time to party. Let's get back to the ballroom."

Thirty minutes later, Johnny Flash grabbed the microphone and approached the front of the stage.

"All right, Kappas," he asked, "are we ready to party?"

Yells, cheers, and loud whistles sounded from the audience.

Johnny continued, "We've had a 45 minute interruption, thanks to your clever rival's L.C.B. trick."

Loud boos and loud curse words blared from the gathering.

Johnny motioning with his hands in an attempt to quiet the Kappas down. "Hold it down," Johnny asked, and then he smiled. "To make up for the 45 minute delay, we are going to play until 2 a.m. instead of one o'clock. Ready for the Beatles show?"

The audience again roared their approval, as the lyrics to *Twist and Shout* blasted out from the ten piece show band. After the song was over, Winston and Desiree returned to their table.

"We were lucky, Brother Beerwolf," Winston smiled as he poured another beer. "Just about all our Brothers and their dates have returned. Those Deltas just about got us good this time."

"We were lucky, Brother Plato," Beerwolf answered, "if you hadn't spotted that truck, this party would have been history."

"That is correct," Winston smiled sadistically.

"You're up to something, Brother Plato," Beerwolf grinned.

"We're going to do the Deltas White Rose in."

"How?" Beerwolf asked.

"We will talk about that at the executive council's special session that I'm calling for next Tuesday night." Winston reached over and kissed Desiree on the cheek. "In the meantime, we have several hours of dancing and partying to tend to."

"This is one hell of a party," Billy The Kid praised as his date and Winston and Desiree walked through the hotel lobby and headed for the elevator hours later.

"Sure was, wasn't it, Desiree?" Winston asked putting his arms around her.

Desiree just nodded her head.

"Can't wait 'til Monday morning, when I walk by the Delta table. They'll have jealousy written all over their faces after they hear about this band. Hell, even Channel 7 showed up to film the band for a short segment on Sunday's ten o'clock news."

The elevator doors opened as the four entered.

"Tired, honey?" Winston asked. "After all, it's 2:30 am."

Desiree stared into Winston's eyes, and kissed his lips softly, "I'm going to be really tired about 3:30, I hope."

Winston grinned.

Chapter

Fifteen

Winston sat at the Kappa Kappa table, debating to himself whether he should make his 10 a.m. class. Desiree, nudged his right leg, "Winston, here comes Michael and Laura."

The two approached the table, as Michael with his hands on his hips stared at the usual morning table occupants. "Well, well, what do we have here?" he smirked, "Stragglers from Gettysburg?"

"Isn't there a factory somewhere that you can go tour?" Winston answered nonchalantly as he lit a cigarette.

"What's the matter, Winston, you don't seem to have a whole lot of zip this morning," Michael made it a point to drag out the word 'zip'.

"Too bad you're little stunt didn't work," Winston grinned as he stared at the duo, "Now it's our turn."

"Don't waste your time, farm boy," Michael cockily smirked.

"As you know, our White Rose this year is at the Diamond Horseshoe, which is completely surrounded by Goodnight Lake except for the one entrance, and we have hired armed guards to patrol all this week and this weekend who would love to shoot themselves a Kappa."

"So?" Winston answered.

"So, farm boy, you haven't a snowball's chance in hell to pull off any tricks on us."

"Doesn't matter, smog breath," Winston replied. "Did you watch the Channel 7 news last night?" Winston stopped to chuckle, "Your White Rose this weekend won't hold a candle to our General's Ball. We had the greatest band to play for any fraternity party anywhere."

"You think so, farm boy." Michael smiled. "Guess who Rocco Orlando has arranged to come to play for us?"

"And who might that be?" Winston asked cynically.

"Ever heard of the famous Drifters?" Michael laughed. "Eat your heart out, Winston 'cause we are going to kick your ass next spring rush." Michael smiled as he guided Laura away from the table. "Your stupid ass General's Ball is going to look like a kindergarten party after our White Rose is held."

"Damn," Dancin' Beerwolf mumbled, "Winston they're going to wipe us out."

"Not looking good," Sgt. T. commented.

"The Drifters are going to play at the White Rose," Brother Rodeo Cool moaned as he spit into his paper cup. "That's going to kick our little dicks in the dirt."

"And they got the number one star in Hollywood coming too," Charlie The Spoon groaned, "and that killer model -

what's her name?"

"Destiny is her name," Brother Horno the Magnificent chimed. "Wow, what a body, what I'd give to. . ."

"Down Horno," Winston warned. "We have a young lady sitting at our table, remember?"

"What are we going to do, Brother Plato?" Brother Sabotage asked.

"I don't know," Winston thought for a moment, "but I will think of something, I always do."

"That's the Kappa Kappa spirit," Brother Beerwolf praised.

"We gotta get these dudes, man," Roll'em Rick encouraged as he stroked his beard and adjusted his dark sunglasses.

"Check out that pair of chicks out there, Rick," Horno pointed out the window at the two girls that were walking down the sidewalk. "Anybody know them?"

Winston just shook his head hopelessly, as he watched Horno get up from his chair and run toward the exit door.

"Like a tiger chasing after two gazelles," Winston observed as he stood up and stretched. "Come on, Desiree, it's time to go."

Chapter

Sixteen

"All right, my fellow Brothers, the executive council is now in session," Winston Fox announced as he banged the gavel on the mahogany table. "Brother Kid, Brother Pens any suggestions on how we can get even with the Deltas?"

Both shook their heads in silence.

"Sgt. T., Spoon, you all have any ideas?" Winston again asked.

No answer again.

"Brother Dancin' Beerwolf, surely you can come up with a plan."

Again, there was silence then Beerwolf said, "I don't know what the hell we can do, they have the only entrance into that supper club heavily guarded with armed security men."

Winston drawled, "Brother Sabotage any suggestions?"

Sabotage remained silent for a few seconds, and then a fire lit in his eyes. "I say we blow the mother up," Sabotage quickly proposed.

"Come on, Brother Sabotage, this is serious shit," Billy pleaded.

"I am serious," Brother Sabotage answered back.

"All right, Brothers," Winston proceeded, "I've got a plan."

"Fire away, Brother Plato," Beerwolf yelled as he started pounding his palms on the table like he was playing drums.

"I've done a little investigative work this afternoon," Winston pause, pleased with himself. "The Deltas have changed their weekend format up a little bit. Friday night, they will have a cocktail hour, followed by a sit down dinner, in which they will hold their award ceremony afterwards," Winston paused to sip on his beer. "Saturday night, will be the biggie, as usual. The Drifters are going to play from 8 p.m. to 1 a.m. Rocco and Destiny are arriving at the airport shortly before 10 a.m. Saturday morning.

"So, what are you getting at?" Sgt. T. asked.

"Sgt. T. and," Winston paused to point his finger at Brother Sabotage, "You, Troy, are going to play soldiers again."

"What the hell are you getting at?" Sgt. T. asked.

"My retired Navy Seal Brother, you and Brother Sabotage are going to scuba dive across that lake sometime after midnight Friday, and you are going to dismantle their heating system where it will be non-functional Saturday night."

"Cool," Sgt. T. replied, "I think you are onto something, oh wise leader."

"Also, there's a blue Northerner blowin' in late Saturday

afternoon," Winston continued. "With no heating system, and all that plate glass overlooking the lake, they will freeze their asses off. There will be no party."

"Sounds like a fun mission to me," Brother Sabotage calmly approved.

"Willie Nelson is doin' some charity benefit Tuesday night at the Diamond Horseshoe," Winston announced. "And Brother Sabotage, and Sgt. T., we are going to attend, so we can scope out the heating system, and get a better picture of the overall layout." Winston paused to sip on his beer, "Brother Beerwolf."

"Yes sir," Beerwolf snapped to attention as he stood up.

"You're job is to acquire all the necessary equipment to make this mission successful."

"Consider it all ready accomplished," Beerwolf answered.

Winston smiled, as he made one final comment, "Just picture the outcome, my fellow Brothers," Winston grinned, "Michael and Laura rushing about, as Rocco and Destiny pace about in confusion. By 8:00 p.m., the temperature in the supper club will be 30 degrees or colder," he laughed. "They'll all be runnin' around like chickens with their heads cut off. I can just see Michael's reaction now." He tried to picture the scene. "Damn it, sure wish I could be there to savor this victory." Winston stood up, and pounded the gavel on the table. "Meeting adjourned."

Four hours later, Winston sat on his bed as usual, staring at the psychedelic posters that lit up the room from the black light above him. "Well, Herman, what do you think, oh boy, think I ought to call Gloria again?" Winston tapped on the aquarium as he looked at Herman.

Herman wiggled back and forth, and for a moment seemed to blow kisses at Winston as his mouth gently touched the glass.

"Well, I guess we can try it again. This time you better be right."

Winston reached down and grabbed a beer from the ice chest. "Here goes," Winston dialed Gloria's number as he anxiously awaited her voice.

"Hello?"

"Hi, Gloria," Winston nervously spoke, "How are you doing?"

"I'm sleeping just fine, thank you for asking."

"I just wanted…"

Before Winston could finish, Gloria interrupts, "Good night, Winston."

Winston again listened to the empty dial tone on the other end, as he admonished Herman. "Wrong again, Herman, oh boy," Winston shook his head in dejection. "Herman, I'm going to have to find me another advisor." Winston just shook his head as he sipped on his beer, "Oh, well, as we both know by now what they say in the old country." Winston paused to take a deep drag from his cigarette, "We're just gonna have to blow that shit off."

Winston sat on his bed and stared at the glowing posters-almost in a trance.

"Herman, Desiree is who I should have called anyway. No need to torture myself, she likes me, and she's not constantly riding my ass."

Winston picked up the phone and dialed her number.

Chapter

Seventeen

The night was very cold and hazy, and unfortunately for the three men that were sitting inside the 1958 Buick not far from Goodnight Lake, a full moon glowed brightly above, illuminating ripples that gently flowed across the lake.

"Damn it," Sabotage griped, "there just had to be a full moon out here tonight."

Sgt. T. sitting in the shotgun seat next to Sabotage, sat silently as he carefully observed the front entrance booth with his high powered army binoculars, then he slowly panned them to the right, focusing his attention on the Diamond Horseshoe Supper Club which was just in front of them, completely encircled by Goodnight Lake, except for the small two lane winding road that curved its way from the entrance booth to the front of the supper club.

"I don't think we need to worry about the moonlight," Sgt. T. commented as he turned his binoculars toward the entrance booth, "no movement over there, those hotshot guards are probably asleep," Sgt. T. paused to open a beer. "Doesn't matter anyway; look at that hazy fog that is rollin' in from the north bank."

"It's eerie out here, that's for sure," Sabotage answered taking a drag from his cigarette as he watched the low rolling fog hover above the lake in front of them, soon only the Diamond Horseshoe's circular windows and roof could be seen by the trio.

"Remember that old Sherlock Holmes movie we watched the other night," asked Brother Beerwolf, sitting in the back seat alone, "what was the name…"

"The Hound of the Baskervilles," Sabotage answered as he listened to a loud howling coming from the small mesa to their right, "but that ain't no hound howling, that's a coyote."

"At least, you hope so," Sgt. T. answered. "Let's get this show on the road, this place is starting to look like the moor in that movie."

"Just like Vietnam, huh, brother Sabotage?" Beerwolf asked as he patted Sabotage on his right shoulder.

"Don't ever mention that word again," Sabotage warned as he glared back at Dancin' Beerwolf.

"Sorry."

"Well, it's going to be a little different mission than I'm used to," Sgt T. smiled as he lit a cigarette.

"What do you mean by that?" Beerwolf asked curiously.

"Instead of dynamiting ships, bridges, and strategic military positions," Sgt. T. paused to grin, "What the hell do you think I'm doin' now but Navy Sealin' it over to a supper club to dismantle a 30 year old heating system."

"Boy, have we really gone downhill," Sabotage commented without cracking a smile.

"Well, let's get this over with," Sgt. T. ordered, "this is cutting into my drinkin' I time…" Sgt. T. turned around and asked Beerwolf, "We got everything we need, Beerwolf - lock picks, waterproof flashlights, and the rest of the list I gave you?"

"It's all right here, ready to go," Beerwolf assured him, "I've doubled checked and triple checked."

"Well, let's get these monkey suits on, and get rollin," Sgt. T. instructed as he opened his car door.

"Damn it's cold," Sabotage griped, "Beerwolf keep an eye on things. I figure it will take us about 15 minutes to get to the club, then maybe 30 minutes or so inside," Sgt. T. paused to lower his goggles over his eyes, "see you in about an hour."

"Good luck, brothers," Beerwolf encouraged.

Twenty five minutes later, the two frogmen stood in front of the huge outdated heating system.

Sgt. T. smiled, "Troy, they're not going to be very happy about all this water we've been splashing on these nice hardwood floors with our fins."

Sabotage smiled as he studied the heater. His flashlight shined on two parts in particular. Removing them carefully, he smiled sadistically, "They haven't got a snowball's chance in hell to find a way to fix this little puppy by tomorrow night. The only way they can is to order the parts back east somewhere," Sabotage paused to chuckle, "Hell, I don't know if they even exist."

Sgt. T. took the two parts from Troy and put them into his waterproof bag. "We mean no harm to toward the club," Sgt. T. commented as the two made their way toward the exit in pitch darkness, "We'll leave these parts on their front entrance

Sunday night."

The two paused before they walked out the back entrance. "Man, this is a magnificent place, stands out here in the middle of this lake like a medieval castle," Sgt. T. praised, "and Troy look out that circular window to our left - the fog has lifted - see those beautiful moon rays shining across the icy water," Sgt. T pointed, "and that full moon above shining through those barren cottonwood trees by the shore."

"Who gives a shit," Sabotage grumbled, "let's get the hell out of here."

Chapter

Eighteen

The front moved in several hours earlier than predicted, producing arctic temperatures, light snow, and wind gusts that at times reached 45 miles per hour. By 8:00 p.m., the temperature had dipped to 11 degrees which was unusually cold even for November, as the snow and wind pounded against the large circular windows at the Diamond Horseshoe Supper Club.

"What do you mean, it can't be fixed?" Michael screamed out in anger at the heating repair man, as he stood by the huge heating system in his black tuxedo.

"I'm sorry, Michael," the old stooped over man apologized but before he could finish, Michael interrupted him. "Sorry, hell," Michael grumbled. "Look over there, I've got the Drifters up there on the stage, one of the most famous bands in the United States. I've got Rocco Orlando sitting over there at that table - the biggest box office star in the country, and they're all freezing their asses off." Michael just shook his head in disbelief as he looked at Laura Love who was standing beside Michael in her lovely black silk evening gown, which was barely visible under the trench coat that she had draped over her cold bare shoulders.

Michael continued his rampage, "I don't believe this shit. I just don't believe it." Michael stared across the room at his Brothers and their dates, who by now had put their coats on, obviously uncomfortable with the temperature in the supper club, which by now had dropped to 19 degrees.

"Christ, man, this is our White Rose, our biggest event of the year," Michael pleaded to the old man. "Hell, we got all the local TV stations comin' at 10:00 p.m. to do a live remote. Even the Today Show crew is coming to film a segment for their Wednesday morning program."

"Michael, look over there," the old man pointed at the heater, "There's two important parts missing."

"What do you mean missing?" Michael asked suspiciously.

"Somebody has sabotaged this heating system." The old man shook his head sadly, "This is an old, old heater, it will take me forever to find these two parts somewhere." The old man pointed over at the large windows, "Those windows are coated with solid ice, and with the lousy insulation in this old building, the temperature will be ten degrees colder in here before the night's over with. I'm afraid you're gonna have to try another time."

"Damn," Michael moaned as he slapped his hands together.

Rocco and Destiny walked over to hear the conversation.

"Sorry, Michael," Rocco offered. "But we're leaving,

this is ridiculous. I promise we'll come back to your spring formal." Rocco shook Michael's hand, "Sorry, pal, bad break, but we're out of here."

Michael watched the two walk away, and shook his head in despair. He walked toward the stage, and was met by the drummer who approached him. The tall good looking black man put his arm on Michael's shoulder, "Sorry, man," he consoled Michael, "but we got African blood in us. I can't handle this West Texas blizzard shit, man. We're goin' have to try this another time, Brother."

Michael kicked the chair in front of him as he turned to Laura, "So the Goddamn Kappas sabotaged this place," Michael threw his fist out in the air like a boxer. "How the hell did they manage to get in here, there's no way they could."

"Sorry, honey," Laura consoled.

"Those soup line bastards have pulled a good one on us this time. They have made fools out of us."

Laura put her hand on Michael's arm, but he shrugged it off.

"Just leave me alone," Michael ordered his temper flaring out of control. "Of all the Podunk Mickey Mouse colleges in the country, I had to end up in this hellhole," Michael just shook his head hopelessly. "Nothin' but a bunch of shit kickers, plow boys, and Johnny Rebs livin' here in this God forsaken pancake piece of shit panhandle. Hell, everybody gets a hard on when they see a fuckin' mesquite tree."

"Michael, please," Laura warned, "This is where I'm from, remember? You're upsetting me with your vulgar remarks."

"Sorry, Laura," Michael apologized. "I didn't mean it. I'm just so frustrated. Hell, we could have been on the Today Show."

Eric Corbyn

Chapter Nineteen

"We could be in Acapulco right now on the beach starin' at the good lookin' chicks," Brother Horno moaned, "But, oh no what are we doing? We're sittin' in a beat up VW minibus in the middle of a West Texas blizzard starin' at a frosted up supper club."

"Cool it, Horno," Winston instructed as he focused his binoculars again on the front entrance to the Diamond Horseshoe Club. "It's after nine now, I figure almost anytime they'll start leaving."

Brother Sabotage who was riding shotgun also continued his observance of the front entrance, with obvious delight. "Freeze, you jerks," Sabotage begged, "I hope you freeze your asses off."

"Look," Sgt. T. pointed toward the entrance not far across

the iced up lake that was between them. "It's Rocco and
Destiny and they're getting into a white limousine."

"And there is Michael and Laura coming out, right behind
them," Brother Charlie The Spoon Luna noted.

"I love it," Winston laughed out loud.

"They are all pouring out now, like rats leaving a sinking
ship," Brother Beerwolf observed as he followed their hasty
exit with binoculars.

"All right, Kappas, time to leave this picnic area, and
beat them to Amarillo," Winston ordered as he headed for the
highway that was less than a half mile ahead. "Hey, Music
Man," Winston called out to Roger who was sitting in the very
back of the van, almost unnoticed, "Play us a tune."

"My name is Roger." Seconds later, Roger wasted no time
inserting a tape into his portable player and the lyrics to a Bob
Dylan classic blasted away, "Johnny is in the basement mixing
up the medicine…"

"All right, Brother Sabotage, let's review our mission -
'Operation Orkin,'" Winston instructed as he turned onto the
icy highway, slowly making his way toward Amarillo. The
snow by now had slackened, but the wind continued to blow,
which made the night ride very uncomfortable.

"Listen carefully," Brother Sabotage requested as he lit a
cigarette, "The Deltas are staying at the newly built Longhorn
Inn just a few miles from here. They have reserved the entire
west wing for their entourage. Even Rocco and Destiny are
staying there, but they will be in the Presidential Suite."

Brother Sabotage paused for a second, popped open a beer
and continued, "Next to this motel there is the recently vacant
Colonial motel which will soon be torn down to make way for
the new Ramada Inn. There's a widow's walk at the top where
I have already placed supplies for us to help our mission."

"What's the mission?" Brother Horno curiously asked.

"The plan is simple, my fellow Brothers," Brother Sabotage stopped - a sinister smile crossed his face. "Sgt. T. and I have carefully placed smoke bombs in the three heating systems in the west wing. When the time is right, we will set them off."

"You gotta be fuckin' kiddin' me dude," Roll em' Rick mumbled as he awakened from his nap.

"Have you ever seen a pile of tires burn?" Sgt. T. asked as he lit a cigarette.

"Sure," Brother Horno answered.

"Well, that's what their rooms are going to look like when that black smoke pours out of those heating vents," Sgt. T. smiled, "Man, will it set off a score of smoke alarms. I figure it will take them less than 30 seconds to flee their rooms in sheer panic. I just hope our timing is right."

"What do you mean by that?" Winston asked.

"I want them fleeing their rooms half naked, but I don't want any of those damn Deltas having enough time to get laid."

Winston smiled as he watched the town lights grow in the distance.

"Also," Brother Sabotage interjected, "We got it rigged where all the floodlights and parking lights will come on when we are ready for them to. After all, we do want to see the fun."

Loud cheers echoed through the van.

Sgt. T. raised his voice over the din, "And as soon as the caravan pulls off the highway we will signal Brother Billy The Kid with a flare who will be parked not far away next to a payphone where he will make three quick calls: one to our lovely Dean of Women, Agnes Peabody, one to our favorite

Dean of Men, J. Strom Goodnight, and one to Brother Wings, who works for Channel 7 News." Sgt. T. paused to glance at his watch, "Hopefully, our timing will be right. We figure it will take them 20 or 30 minutes to show up after we have tipped them a little prematurely that nearly a hundred of their students are about to burn to death in a motel fire."

Winston added, "Also with a little luck, we'll have all the Delta Phi's and their dates runnin' about in bright lights, half naked with everybody showing up including the fire trucks and the police. It will look like a three ring circus if everything works out right."

Winston turned onto the access road and headed for the back of the vacant Colonial motel. "We're here," Winston said, "and there's Billy's minibus parked over there waiting for our signal."

Ten minutes later, Sgt. T., Brother Sabotage, and Winston climbed the outdoor ladder up to the widow's walk.

"Perfect observation tower, Sgt. T.," Winston noted as he removed the three army field binoculars from the backpack that Brother Sabotage had brought up the night before along with blankets and other supplies. The trio knelt quietly against the wooden rail and observed carefully the motel's west wing.

"They should be about here, it's after ten," Winston commented as he pointed his binoculars toward the highway.

"Here comes Rocco's white limo now, it's turning off."

"Damn it's cold," Brother Sabotage moaned, as he crawled over to a maze of wires that were tangled up in the corner not far from where the trio had perched. Returning two minutes later, he assured the other two, "All systems ready to go."

"Here comes our little Delta Phi caravan now," Sgt. T. observed as he watched the long procession proceed down the access road, and then slowly turn into the motel entrance. Ten minutes later the motel parking lot was full.

"Get your asses up to your rooms, boys," Winston urged.

"Well, there goes Rocco and Destiny up to their Presidential Suite," Sgt. T. observed, "and check the couple going up the right hand stairs. It's the Italian stallion and the lovely traitor Laura Love. Boy, are you all in for a surprise."

"And look whose getting out of that white Corvette," Sgt. T. pointed to the left. "If it isn't Bambi. Wonder who is the lucky one that she's with tonight?"

The trio continued to observe the gathering until the last two couples parked and headed for their rooms. One minute later, Brother Sabotage sent a low flying red flare signaling Billy to make his three calls.

"It's now ten o'clock," Brother Sabotage noted, "in exactly twenty-five minutes, we will set the smoke bombs off."

The trio watched nervously, noticing light after light being switched off until the motel's west wing was in almost total darkness. The snow continued, but it was light and blew nearly sideways because of the heavy wind.

Brother Sabotage checking his watch scooted over to the wiring, and began to fumble with them. "Bingo," Brother Sabotage mumbled out loud, "All systems go. Get ready."

The three watched the rooms with eagerness, awaiting the first exit from the smoke filled rooms. Three minutes passed, as the trio awaited in nervous anticipation.

"What's the damn holdup?" Winston griped, "Is something…"

Before he could finish, a door swung open on the second floor. The door went flying over the rail, crashing into a car windshield below.

"Here they come," Sgt. T. observed, "they are pouring out

of their rooms like cockroaches."

"God look at that black smoke billow out of those open doors," Winston instructed, "it looks like a volcano eruption."

Sabotage scooted quickly over to the wires and fumbled with them again. Seconds later, lyrics from Jimmy Hendrix's *All Along the Watchtower* blared loudly, "There must be some way out of here, said the joker to the thief."

"What the hell?" Winston blurted out as Sabotage approached him.

"Thought we would have a little music to add to the night's entertainment."

"But how?" Winston started to ask.

Sabotage just smiled, "Roger went with me last night. All it took was an old tape deck and a little trick wiring to a loudspeaker."

"Look to your left," Sgt. T. instructed, "look who is dashing out of the Presidential Suite."

"I'll be damned," Winston grinned, "here comes Rocco in his silk robe and Destiny in her nightgown - both barefooted, running down the stairs."

Winston turned the binoculars to room 269 where Michael and Laura were staying, "Anybody seen Michael yet?"

"Not yet," Sgt. T. answered, "but look to your right, there's Buffy hopping about in her panties holding a pillow over her chest."

"Don't bother to cover up those tiny tits," Brother Sabotage, sarcastically commented, "nobody wants to see them anyhow."

"Be nice, Brother," Winston said, "look at her hoppin' about in the cold snow. She looks like a rooster on acid."

In the background, another song blasted out into the

night.

"There is a house in New Orleans, they call it the Rising Sun, and it's been the ruin…"

"What a great song by the Animals," Winston smiled, "*The House of the Rising Sun*, and how suitable for the night, oh Roger."

"Hey Brothers," Sgt. T. whispered, "check out room 269. Here comes the Italian Stallion and our little traitor Laura Love."

"Look at them," Winston laughed as he zeroed in his binoculars on the escaping couple, "Laura's got on only her bra and her panties, bright red ones, I might add, and look at Michael running about with that hot dog skimpy underwear he's wearing. How embarrassing Michael, oh boy."

The trio all smirked as they watched the two dash out into the parking area. Soon the whole lot was filled with Deltas and their dates, wondering what to do. Bambi, with only a sheet wrapped around her, rushed over to Michael. "Michael what the hell is going on?" She screamed in panic, "Damn it, my feet are freezing."

"The motel is on fire," Michael answered as he rubbed his cold hands together back in forth. "Look at that black smoke pourin' out of those open doors, the whole damn motel is on fire." Michael turned and hollered out as loud as he could yell, "All right, Brothers, everybody make a dash for the lobby over there."

"But, Michael," Laura said her face shivering in the extreme cold, "We can't, it's gotta be on fire to."

"Well, it's either that, or freeze to death," Michael uttered.

"To your left, Brothers," Sgt. T. instructed, "Look who just drove up just in the nick of time. If it isn't J. Strom and that little bitch Agnes getting out of the same car."

"Perfect timing, I believe," Brother Sabotage smirked, "I see I haven't lost my touch." Brother Sabotage then scooted over to the wiring. "Time for a little light show, my Brothers."

Seconds later, the parking area lit up like a Christmas tree, at the same time, the lyrics from a great Bob Dylan classic blasted in the background, "Once upon a time, you dressed so fine, threw the bums a dime in your prime, didn't you?"

"Another perfect song for the occasion, Brother," Winston praised, "hope you all can hear it, where you are."

The trio continued to observe the action below them.

"Hey," Sgt. T. pointed to his left, "here come the Channel 7 News truck driving in. Thank you, Brother Wings."

"And listen to those sirens coming from the fire trucks and police squad cars coming down the highway," Winston hooted, "and all those smoke alarms blaring."

"Yeah, well I wish they wouldn't be so damn loud," Brother Sabotage moaned, "I can barely hear my favorite song."

Dylan's lyrics continued to blast out into the cold night, "how does it feel to be on your own, like a complete unknown, with no direction known, like a rolling stone."

J. Strom and Agnes rushed toward the confused and screaming students. "What the hell is going on, Michael?" Strom asked as he stared at the gathering - some girls topless, guys in their underwear, and some wearing sheets wrapped tightly around their bodies. "What the hell are we having here - a toga party in the snow?" J. Strom slapped his hands together in disgust, "and where the hell is that music coming from? Turn that crap off, and for Godsakes, get some Goddamn clothes on."

Michael stood sheepishly in his skimpy underwear trying to shield Laura's appearance. "Dr. Goodnight," Michael replied, "look at that black smoke - the whole damn motel is in flames."

"Laura," Agnes lectured, "my God, look at you and your sorority sisters, I am so ashamed of all of you," Agnes just shook her head back and forth. "This is the most embarrassing incident that I have ever witnessed in my 22 year tenure as Dean of Women at WTSU. My God, what are you having, an orgy?"

Laura did not answer, instead she turned toward Michael, with tears streaming from her eyes, and ripped off her fraternity drop necklace and threw it at Michael's face. "Michael, damn you," she cried out in hopelessness, "you have ruined us all."

"But, Laura, honey, it's not my fault," Michael begged, "I didn't start this fire, but I bet you I know who did."

Rocco and Destiny worked their way over the frozen parking lot to where Michael and company were.

"Where the hell is our limo driver, Willie?" Rocco asked Destiny.

"I don't know," Destiny answered as she danced her feet back and forth, "do something, Rocco, I'm freezing to death."

"Get that Goddamn camera out of my face," Rocco warned the Channel 7 newsman who had approached them, "or I will break your neck, you understand?"

Brother Wings backed away quickly, but still focused his camera on the happenings.

"Goddamn it, Michael," J. Strom shouted at him. "Your fraternity is through at WTSU, this little fiasco is going to cost us a fortune in alumni support, and with all these damn TV stations here, we're going to be the laughing stock of the nation - particularly with Rocco here." J. Strom kicked the snow in hopelessness. "My God, another damn fire truck," J. Strom moaned, "whose coming next, the whole damn town?"

"Somebody turn that music off, please," Agnes ordered. "Where the dickens is it coming from, and turn those floodlights off."

Dylan's lyrics continued to blast out, "now you don't look so proud having to scrounge for your next meal, how it feels…"

"Everyone quickly follow me to the snack bar by the pool," a tall lanky man ordered as he approached the gathering, with several of his motel staff following him carrying blankets, passing them out to the begging guests. "Come on," he urged, "you will get warm in there, it's heated."

"Damn, I wish I knew what all was being said down there between J. Strom and Michael, and everybody else," Winston moaned.

"Who cares," Brother Sabotage answered, "let's get the hell out of here, pronto. Billy should have picked up the others by now, and is waiting for us in the parking area at the Palo Duro motel just across the street."

"Let's get all this stuff in this duffle bag," Sgt. T. directed, "don't want to leave any evidence behind."

"Keep low," Sabotage warned as he gathered up the wires, in the process cutting the wires to the floodlights that lit up the Longhorn Inn parking area, "let's get the hell out of here, or the police will be on us like a duck on June bugs."

Five minutes later, the trio approached Brother Billy's minibus, boarding it as fast as they could.

"Hey, my fellow Kappas, " Billy started to speak.

"Not now, Kid," Brother Sabotage ordered, "let's haul ass, we'll shoot the shit later."

Billy without hesitation guided the minibus away from the action ahead, taking the back road toward Washington Street which would eventually get them on the highway well on their way to Taos.

Minutes later, Winston sighed a sign of relief, "Thank goodness, I think we are out of the danger zone now." Winston quickly lit up a cigarette.

"Got a little surprise for you, Brother Plato," Billy smiled, as he pointed down the aisle to Desiree, who was walking up the aisle.

"Hi, Winston," Desiree spoke in her soft seductive voice, "what's you been doing?"

Winston hugged her and then laughed out loud, "Are you coming with us to Taos?"

"Of course, I can't wait to meet the famous Brother Surf, and I have never been to Taos," Desiree smiled as she kissed Winston hard on the lips.

"How did it go?" Brother Horno The Magnificent asked, eagerly awaiting an answer.

"Mission accomplished," Brother Sabotage calmly stated, "you all should have been there - all those chicks running around nearly naked, J. Strom and Agnes showing up just at the right time," Sabotage paused to laugh, "and then the TV crews showed up."

"We couldn't have planned it any better," Sgt. T. smirked as he took a long drag from his cigarette, "and to see Laura Love run around in her panties and see through bra…"

Before he could finish, Brother Horno horned in, "In her see through bra cold as it was out there?"

"That's correct, hyena breath," Winston laughed, "Eat your heart out."

"All right, Brothers," Brother Billy warned as he turned onto the highway, "we have a long night ahead of us, best I can figure if we are lucky, we will reach Taos by daybreak.

In the meantime, Brother Beerwolf, get our newly boarded passengers some chips and beer."

"Yes, sir," Beerwolf answered as he headed back toward the keg.

"And Brother Roll'em Rick," Billy laughed, "You just remain in a stupor for awhile until you wake up."

"Hey man, I know what's happening, dude," Roll'em answered, as he sat quietly adjusting his sunglasses.

"Don't you ever take those damn things off?" Brother Beerwolf asked.

"Like why should I, man?" Roll'em mumbled as he bowed his head and slumped farther down in his seat.

"Can't wait to watch the 12 o'clock news tomorrow, drinking beers with Surf," Winston smiled, "and Surf is furnishing us an alibi."

"What do you mean?" Desiree asked.

"He has registered us in for tonight," Winston answered with a grin, "anybody tries to pin this on us, all we have to say is that we were on a ski trip in Taos."

"Right on, Brother Plato!" Beerwolf hollered, "Beers anyone?"

"You think we can make it in this weather, Winston?" Sgt. T. asked with concern.

"Oh, hell," Winston answered, "if we don't all it can do is kill us." Winston paused and hugged Desiree and kissed her on the cheek. "Well, Brothers, we're off to Taos, and we have a cover, because the University's elite will be dogging us big time. The shit is really going to hit the fan this time. They are going to be after us like never before."

"Do you think we went too far?" Billy asked as he guided the minibus down the snow packed highway.

"Well, if we did, Brother Billy," Winston calmly replied as he took a long sip from his 32 ounce beer cup, "You know what they say in the ol' country, don't you?"

In unison, all the Brothers, except Roll' em, yelled out, "You just gotta blow that shit off."

"Right on," Rodeo Cool hollered, at the same time, spilling his spit cup on Gretchen's left shoe. "Damn it, Billy take those curves easy, man."

"Oh, Rodeo, honey," Gretchen pleaded, "sure wish you would quit that nasty habit."

"All right, Music Man, a little traveling music," Winston requested, as he looked back down the aisle at Roger, who as usual sat unnoticed in the very back of the bus.

"My name is Roger," The Music Man calmly reminded as he reached into his 8-track case and proceeded to plug in a tape into his 8-track cassette player. Soon the lyrics from the great Animals classic *We Gotta Get Out Of This Place* began playing.

"Perfecto," Brother Plato congratulated as he turned his attention to Desiree, "and honey, if it's the last thing we ever do, we gotta get out of this place. Girl, there's a better life for you and me."

Soundtrack

California Dreamin' by the Mamas and the Papas
Born to be Wild by Steppenwolf
With a Little Help from My Friends by the Beatles
Riders in the Sky by the Doors
Start Me Up by the Rolling Stones
Gloria by Van Morrison
Satisfaction by the Rolling Stones
Stayin' Alive by the Bee Gees
Limbo Rock by Chubby Checker
Light My Fire by the Doors
Black Magic Woman by Santana
Yesterday by the Beatles
Brown Sugar by the Rolling Stones
Jumpin' Jack Flash by the Rolling Stones
Honky Tonk Women by the Rolling Stones
Twist and Shout by the Top Notes
Positively 4th Street by Bob Dylan
All Along the Watchtower by Bob Dylan
House of the Rising Sun by the Animals
Like a Rolling Stone by Bob Dylan
We Gotta Get Out of This Place by the Animals

CPSIA information can be obtained
at www.ICGtesting.com
Printed in the USA
FFOW05n0008040414